I0566568

Backdoor Tales

VOLUME II

AN EROTIC SHORT STORY ANTHOLOGY

EMILY ROOKS

True Lust

BACKDOOR TALES
AN EROTIC SHORT STORY ANTHOLOGY

Copyright Emily Rooks, 2025

A Production of True Lust

ISBN 978-1-948872-43-0

Manufactured in the United States of America
First printing July 2025

Contents

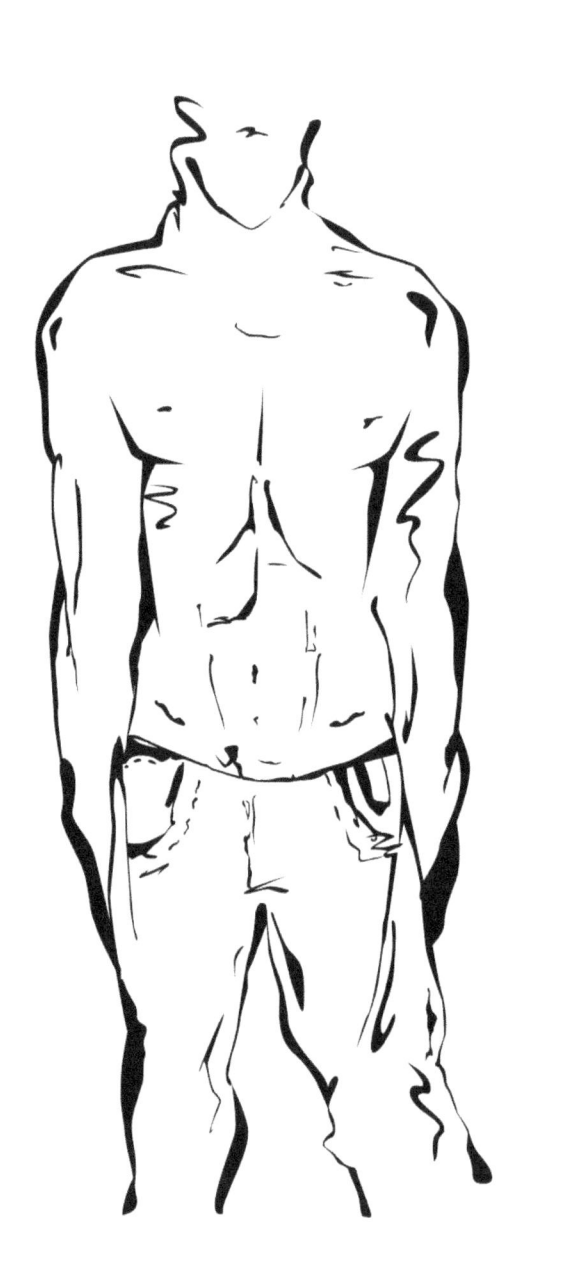

All the Way

I meant to keep on going, right down to Nashville, but I got his call out near Ashland, so I was close enough to turn around. After all, it was Bobby.

"Johanna and I got into a bad fight," my brother-in-law said with a drawl, "can I crash at your place tonight?"

"What are you two arguing about now?" I asked as looking for a place to whip a uey.

"What else, Candace? Money."

What else, indeed. "You two are always arguing about money."

"You know how your sister is."

Yeah, I knew. "All right, I'll be there in a couple of hours."

"No problem. Oh, and Candace – thanks. I'm sorry to ruin your trip."

I was just glad he was a Florida transplant or he'd be moving back in with one of his family. It'd be much better to have his cute little ass in my place for a night or two.

I checked my speed. Ohio State Highway Patrol be damned. I stepped on the accelerator until my speed hit 80.

***

Eight years ago...

With all the lights turned off, we waited silently as the porn movie began. None of us girls had seen a full-length porno before – sure, we'd seen snippets and short reels given away

1

free online – but we wanted to know how anyone could turn sex into a 90-minute film. Guess that tells you what kind of guys we'd dated.

Glimpses of hunky men, moaning women, and hot sex punctuated the opening credits, leaving all of us raising our eyebrows as grinning. Soon the scenes had us giggling nervously then making lewd comments that left us laughing; if not for the high pitch of our voices, you might've thought we were a bunch of sailors.

I won't lie, the movie got me a little tingly despite how dumb it was. But then something came on the screen that totally changed me.

The hunky guy, while eating out Kitty Rose – why do only female porn stars have names? – placed his palms under her thighs and lifted her legs up and back toward her head, fully exposing her ass to him. His tongue moved down her taint to the netherhole and circled it then dipped in. A collective "Eww!" went up from the girls, but I found myself staring at his ministrations and suddenly breathing more deeply. Two seconds later, realizing I was the only one having that reaction, I faked a grimace and said "Yuck."

Thankfully everyone else wanted to see just how grossed out they could get, so we kept watching – and I kept pretending to not show much interest, though I memorized every moment.

Then the hunky guy pulled back, slapped Kitty Rose's butt and told her to get on all fours. As she did, he grabbed a bottle of lube and poured a more than liberal amount upon her butt crack and along his impressively large cock. He got on his knees behind her and guided his member to her netherhole and pressed.

2

Kitty Rose let out a groan of pleasure, and he kept working his way into her, until he was half-buried in her ass. My mouth was open wide, and I couldn't take my eyes off the screen, as he pumped in and out of her.

Makenzie play elbowed me. "I think you like this."

That broke my attention, and I shook my head. "Uh, no…" *Think fast*, I told myself. "…I can't believe she can take a cock that big in her."

"Riight?" said Elizabeth on the other side of me. "That's got to be painful."

What was painful was the ache in my pum-pum. If just a guy and me had been watching this, I'm sure I would have pulled off my panties and opened wide for him.

After hunky man came in Kitty Rose's ass, they kissed, and the movie was over. Every one decided they needed to leave my apartment near Tri-C, a few alleging an early class the next day. I made sure not many lights went on as everyone left, for I wasn't sure if the wetness soaking my panties had seeped through my jeans front.

I don't think I ever came so quickly or so hard as when I masturbated once all were gone.

***

Bobby sat atop his car, using the windshield for a back rest, as I pulled in. Despite being early September, the late summer heat wave still gripped Cleveland.

"Waiting long?" I said.

"Since I called," Bobby said in his slight Floridian drawl. He shrugged. "Need me to carry your bags up?"

Bobby was a gentleman. How could my sister not appreciate that? But I had to decide if I was going to Nashville anytime

3

soon. Hopefully not. "That'd be great," I said.

He lugged the two duffel bags on his shoulders as following me.

Once inside, I turned on the air and went to the cupboard. "Bet you could use a drink?" I said.

He nodded, his shaggy, dirty-blond hair flopping about as he did, and I poured two whiskeys on ice for us.

"Thought you liked your whiskey neat," he said as taking the glass I offered.

"It's too hot in here not to have ice."

He laughed. Bobby had a good sense of humor. How could my sister not appreciate that?

We sat on opposite ends of the couch, his bright, citrus fragrance wafting on the AC's currents toward me. "Tell me all about it," I said.

"As you know, I make more than Johanna."

"Yet another example of gender inequality." I grinned.

He rolled his eyes good naturedly. Damn, those rich chocolate brown eyes of his looked good. "So we agreed that since I earn 60% of our combined income, I should pay 60% of the bills and she 40%."

"Sounds reasonable. Except if I recall it took you six months of arguing to agree to that."

Bobby grimaced. "So now she says that her paying 40% eats up too much of her income, doesn't give her enough left over to meet her personal needs."

"I can see that. So why doesn't she get a better paying job?"

"That's what I said!"

"Let me guess – that's what you *shouldn't* have said."

"Exactly. She told me *I* should get a better paying job."

4

"That would mean you make, say 65% of the combined income, so she only has to pay 35%, which gives her more money for her personal needs."

"Does that seem fair?"

"I bet she said you wouldn't be spending all of that extra 5% you earn on bills, so you'll also have more money for your personal needs, right?"

"How did you know? She said it's a win-win."

"I had a similar argument with her over gas money in high school."

"The thing is I like my job. I have responsibility but low stress. And I'm good at what I do. A higher-paying position just means doing what I don't want to do and more ass-kissing the bosses."

I went to the kitchen and brought the whiskey bottle back to the coffee table. "We're going to need more of this, aren't we?"

***

Eight years ago, after the porn film...

I suddenly found myself watching movies featuring hetero anal sex – on my cell phone, on my laptop, on my television – when by myself. Don't get the idea I was watching them 24/7. It was just every once in a while, whenever I got the urge to be with a guy. I'd start thinking about how turned on I got watching that Kitty Rose film and out of curiosity would want to learn more about it.

Most of the films on porn sites geared toward men were about exerting power over the woman, even humiliating her. When not done that way, they still could be a turn on. Fortunately, I found a couple of sites geared toward women, and there the films focused on more of an erotic coupling, of a loving experience based on intimacy and exploration.

In a few instances, I even copied, as best I could, the rimming experience by wetting my fingertip and running it around my netherhole. I'd never felt such intense stimulation.

But it left me confused.

Though the films and experiencing my own self-pleasure seemed natural, I'd never talked about anal sex in high school health classes or with doctors or even among my friends. It was viewed as taboo. Thanks to this stigma, I knew next to nothing about it except what I saw in those few escapist films.

And that meant my interest remained a secret.

***

Eventually the AC cooled the place, and the liquor left us feeling relaxed. Conversation turned to everyday life, the latest TV shows we were watching, shared memories of good times together when I had a boyfriend and the four of us did things together. Night had fallen, and just crumbs remained of the pizza we had ordered.

"When are you going to get a new boyfriend so we can start doing stuff as couples again?" Bobby said.

"Thinking of getting back together with Johanna? This afternoon, you were considering a divorce."

His eyes fell to the floor. "I'm afraid divorce is where it's going to end up."

I reached over and caressed his arm. "I'm sorry."

He nodded then rose. "Suppose I should be getting to bed. I'm going into work for a couple of hours tomorrow morning to fill in for Dangelo. Blankets and pillow still in the hallway closet?"

I stood up, a little wobbly, and gripped his upper arm. His

muscles felt more solid than I thought they would. "Bobby, you don't have to sleep on the couch."

Our eyes met, and a moment later, our faces moved toward one another.

Then he pulled back. "I'm sorry, Candace, I can't. I do really like you, but...well, I am still mar–"

"I get it," I quick said before he could finish that one word I didn't want to hear him say. "Sorry. Yeah, it's all in the hallway closet."

I watched him walk to it, admiring – like I'd done a thousand times before – the way his ass filled his jeans. My toes always curled at the sight. When he turned back, I grabbed the pizza box and brought it to the garbage can.

"Sweet dreams," I said.

***

Three years ago...

Johanna and I sat out on the deck overlooking the river at Collision Bend. I had a whiskey neat, and she was nursing some fruity little thing.

"Bobby got me flowers last night," she said. "A whole bouquet of them; they look like they're exploding out of the vase."

I smiled. For the past year, she'd been dating him, a real hunk who she sometimes treated like shit, if only because she was good looking enough to get away with it. On the plus side, Johanna and I had gotten along better than ever since she started dating him; I chalked it up to us realizing as young adults how precious sisterhood was. On the minus side, my heart thumped hard every time she said Bobby's name.

"What about that Gabriel?" she teased. "Things seem to be getting serious."

"Yeah, it's been a year now."

She held up her hand, and the afternoon sun glinted off her diamond engagement ring. A couple of women at a neighboring table gazed jealously at it. "Took me two years for Bobby to give this to me. Don't wait much longer than that, okay 'lil sis?"

"Well, there's a problem..."

Her eyes went back to me. "Oh no. Do tell."

"It's nothing about him or us, well not exactly. You see, before I marry anyone, I've always wanted to...well..."

Her hand settled on my arm, caressed it. "What's wrong, Candace?"

"Well, have you and Bobby, ever had...well..."

"Sex?" She laughed. "Of course. Are you saying you and Gabriel haven't?"

"No, we've had it, but..."

"You didn't enjoy it? He's no good at it?"

"No, no, not that at all. The sex is fine. It's just that I crave something...*more*."

Her brow crinkled. "*More?* Like how?"

"Well, have you and Bobby ever tried..." I looked down as my face reddened. "...anal sex?"

Her face firmed. "No, and if Bobby did try, the nearest heavy object would become one with his head. Is this Gabriel trying to force you to have anal sex with him?"

"No, not at all."

"What is it then?"

"*I* want to have anal sex with him."

8

Her face firmed, like that of a principal who'd just caught you running down the hallway. She leaned toward me, whispered, "Keep it down. You don't want anyone to hear *that*."

I lowered my voice. "How do you think I should approach him about it?"

"You *shouldn't*."

"Why?"

"Oh Candace, where did you ever get such a filthy mind? Because anal sex is *dirty*, that's why. You know what comes out of that end, don't you?"

"Yes, but–"

"If you talk to Gabriel about it, he'll think you're a weirdo and break up with you. Not that I would blame him either."

"What!"

She whispered just loud enough for me to hear. "Anal sex isn't something *normal* people do."

"A lot of people do it. And I read an article online about how it can be done so it's not unhealthy or painful–"

Johanna rolled her eyes. "Oh, the Internet, well then!" She quick downed her drink. "I need to go. I can't believe we're having this discussion." She stood up.

And with that, I never spoke about it again to her.

***

Bobby left the next morning for work and didn't come back the entire afternoon. I hesitated to text him...he was a grown man, after all, and what he was doing wasn't any of my business. So I made a lunch for myself that I also could quick throw together for him should he return. I called Alyssia to apologize for not coming down to Nashville and asked for a rain check. Later, I made sure there were leftovers from dinner, presuming he would spend another night at my place. For all I knew, though, he and Johanna had made up.

What the fuck am I doing? I asked myself. *I should be in Nashville right now, looking for a new job. I shouldn't have run back here just because he called. How desperate am I?*

He showed up around seven that night, as the sun was setting over C-Town.

"Hey," I said from the couch and set down my book.

"Hey." He took a seat at the other end.

"How was your day?"

"After work, I just wandered around and thought a lot."

"About what?"

"Johanna. My unhappiness. Us."

When he said *us* I almost gulped. "That's a lot to think about it. What did you decide?"

"That it's all over between Johanna and me. I can't be happy with her. The time has come to move on."

I nodded. "How do you feel about that?"

"Oddly, I feel like it's freeing. As if a great amount of stress has just been let out of me."

I nodded, waiting for him to continue.

Instead, he picked up the remote control from the coffee table. "Wanna watch something?"

"Not until you finish."

"Huh?"

"You said you thought about my sister, about your unhappiness, and about *us*. You told me about Johanna and your unhappiness but not *us*."

"I was going to get to that while watching TV."

10

Mhm...was he going to put some move on me? "Tell me before we watch TV."

"I wish your sister was more like you."

And I wish my boyfriends were more like you. "I think last night you told me everything I needed to know."

"Last night I was confused. Today, it's all a lot clearer."

I hesitated then finally said it. "Not for me."

His brow furrowed.

"I'm glad you spent the day thinking about it. I spent the whole day thinking about you. But you never texted me about where you were, if you were coming back here for lunch or dinner, if you were even coming back at all."

"It's not like we're, well you know."

"*Married?* Christ, Bobby, I was on my way to Nashville but turned around for you." Shit, he was no different than Gabriel.

"Look, I'm sorry about last night. I made a mistake. My head wasn't in a good place."

It hasn't been in a good place since you met Johanna. I huffed and stood up. "I'm tired of waiting."

"You don't have to wait anymore."

"You've said that before!"

I took off for my bedroom, hoping he got a good view of my ass just so he knew what he was missing, then slammed the door behind me.

He didn't come to make up.

Fuck him.

***

Two years ago...

In Gabriel, I finally found a man I could trust. Not that opening up to him about my fetish was easy. But after years of

11

fantasizing about it, I had to try it, Johanna's advice be damned.

Through dinner at the Noble Beast, though, I kept wiping my clammy hands against my jeans and telling myself that saying nothing probably was best.

"You look nervous," he said. "Is everything all right?"

Well, he's called; have to show my cards now or go home. I set down my fork. "Actually yeah. There's something I want to talk about."

He stopped eating his porkstrami sandwich despite how damn good it looked, reached for my hand, and held it. "What is it, honey?" he said gently.

"I have kind of a personal question. Have you ever had anal sex?" My face reddened.

His brow furrowed. "No...why do you ask?"

"I've always wanted to try it. Would you be interested?"

His face kind of blanched for a moment then he seemed to recover. "Um, yeah, I'll try it with you."

Instant relief flooded over me.

Then he quick said, "Have *you* ever tried it?"

I stiffened. "No. I just was curious about it. It's not something I would do with anyone – it would have to be someone I can trust."

He squeezed my hand then went back to his porkstrami. "That means a lot to me. You can trust me."

I nodded. Somehow his last sentence didn't seem too convincing, but I chalked it up to my nerves. "I mean it."

Gabriel nodded then slowly said, "When would you like to try it?"

I took a long breath. "Tonight."

***

You should never spend the night alone in your bedroom while the man you love is asleep on your living room couch. But my anger kept me from opening that door despite my tossing and turning.

The scent of brewing coffee – strong just the way I like it – finally lured me from the bedroom to the kitchen. Streams of sunlight made their way through the edges of the blinds, as I took a seat on a high-top chair at the bar separating the kitchen from the living room.

"How much for a cup of coffee?" I said.

Bobby turned around, all smiles. *Good, maybe this is going to be easy.* "It's your coffee, and your coffeemaker, and let's see, your coffee cup, so free!"

I grinned, as he handed me a steaming cup. My eyes fluttered open at the first sip.

"Say, I'm sorry about last night," I said. "I shouldn't have stormed away mad."

"For a minute there last night, I thought I was with Johanna."

"No need to get nasty."

He sipped from his cup. "I probably should look around today for an apartment."

Something in my stomach dropped. "There's no rush. You're welcome to stay here."

"I appreciate that. But it'll all be less complicated if I'm in my own place."

"What's so complicated? You said you had thought through things yesterday."

"I had. Then I thought through things last night."

"Well I did too."

He turned to the refrigerator, opened it. "Say do you have an creamer?"

"You know I would never lower myself by having creamer, so quit avoiding the subject."

He came back to his side of the bar. "You caught me there."

"Look, I was doubting myself all night. I'm willing to figure it out – how it would work between me and you."

He slowly shook his head and looked away then came back to my eyes. "Like I said, that complicates things."

After a night of anger, I had no energy left in me to reason with anyone. "You really want to…get your own place?"

"Maybe after everything settles with Johanna–"

"And how long will that be?" I said with a little edge. The coffee was starting to kick in.

"I don't know," he said raising his voice. "Christ, you can't do this to me, Candace. You go to bed hating me, the next morning you can't live without me."

My body leaned back a little. I'd never really seen him angry before. "I'm sorry."

"Me too. I'll be back this evening to get my stuff. Dangelo said they're openings in his complex, and I'll just crash at his place tonight." He dumped his coffee into the sink then headed for the front door.

He didn't stomp out. But he might as well had, because crushed was how my heart felt.

***

Two years ago, after dinner…

My pum-pum pulsed with each curl of Gabriel's tongue over my clit, and breathless, I grasped at the sheets. Then a blaze of pleasure swept through my whole body as I bucked against his face and screamed. My jerking eased as the fire slowly left my body. It was usually how we had sex – he made me cum first that took care of himself. I had no complaints.

"Wow – that was fantastic," I said after catching my breath. "I think the anticipation of what is going to happen next really excited me."

He nodded. "Are you sure you want to do this?"

I sat up on my elbows and nodded. "Yeah."

"How do we start?"

"You've seen it in videos, haven't you?"

He shrugged. "How do *you* want me to start?"

"Rimming?" I'd specially cleaned myself up down there for him.

Gabriel hesitated for a moment, and I pulled my legs back, lifting my ass off the mattress, fulling exposing my tight netherhole to him. He leaned forward, licked my taint then ran his tongue in broad circles across my butt cheeks, circling the hole.

I murmured in pleasure. but he kept focusing on the butt cheeks. "Try to get closer to my hole," I said.

His circle tightened but still largely swabbed my taint and cheeks.

"Get your tongue right up to its edge."

He pulled back. "I don't really feel comfortable doing that."

"You will when you hear the sounds I'm going to make once you do get that close."

He stood. "Maybe we could…"

I sat up, got a good look at his magnificent cock bobbing before him. I couldn't wait for him to fill me with it. "Sure, it's okay." Climbing off the bed, I leaned over it, spread my legs so he could take me at the right angle. "Be sure to use plenty of lube."

He didn't move for a couple of seconds – *probably admiring the sexiness of me being in this vulnerable position*, I told myself – then took the lube bottle and squeezed it so ample amounts fell onto my butt crack and slid down it. His hand caught any that would have dripped onto the carpet, as he lubed his fingers.

Gabriel brought one of his fingers to my netherhole and ran it around my rim. A shiver of pleasure swept through me. I let go a soft moan.

Then he pulled back his finger. "Sorry. I can't do this."

I wiggled my butt. "Sure you can. Just press your finger in – slowly. I know you would never hurt me."

"No, Candace," he said, a little firmer, "I really can't do this."

I stood up, faced him. "What's wrong?"

"Look, real men don't have anal sex."

"What?" *Those guys on the porn videos sure looked real to me.*

"Anal sex is something gay guys do."

"Gay guys aren't real men, is that what you're saying?"

"No, that's not, and you know it. I mean real hetero men don't do anal sex."

A lead weight felt like it'd dropped in my stomach. 'That's nonsense. What about those men in porn videos who do women anally?"

"C'mon, Candace, they're getting paid to do that."

I teasingly played with his chest hair, then said in a sultry voice, "How much do you want me to pay you, big boy?"

He grimaced and stepped away. "It grosses me out, frankly. And just *why* do you want to do it anyway?"

My sexy smile turned to a frown. *Okay, this is a lost cause tonight.* I took his hand. "It's all right, forget about it. Here, I'll bend over the bed, and you can take me from behind in the pum-pum."

"Actually, I don't think I'm interested anymore."

"Not interested in fucking me?" I glanced at his half-deflated dick. *He really isn't.* "Oh, don't be like this, Gabriel."

"Be like what?" he said, his brow squinched and eyes glaring. "I'm going home."

"Home?" *Oh fuck.*

I watched him dress quickly then head out the front door. During dinner, he said he would try this with me. I expected a little awkwardness with it being our first time, but I didn't expect him to be angry and leaving me alone.

Little did I know.

***

The knock at the door awoke me from my Netflix trance. I hadn't expected to see Bobby that night and figured it must be Johanna. She hadn't texted or phoned me since Bobby came over, so the time had come for her to either search for or bitch about him.

Looking through the keyhole, though, there was Bobby's unmistakable shaggy, dirty-blond hair.

I quick undid the chain lock then opened the door. "Bobby!"

His head was down, looking at the landing. "Mind if I stay another night?"

I stepped aside to let him in. "What happened?"

"Applied for an apartment over at Dangelo's complex. But it'll be Monday before they get back to me. And Dangelo has a girl over, so…"

"You're welcome to stay here," I said as closing the door,

"but I don't expect you to storm out on me again like you did this morning."

He turned to face me. "You mean like you did to me last night?"

"Touche. Okay, I won't."

His voice softened. "Me either."

"Have you heard from Johanna?"

"No, have you?"

I shook my head.

"Don't try talking me into calling her."

My hands went to my waist. "What makes you think I would?"

"So you can have your place to yourself tonight."

My mouth fell. "I skipped out on going to Nashville for you."

"Look, I don't want to fight. That makes me feel like I'm with Johanna again."

"You take that back." When he said nothing, I stomped my foot. "Take it back, *right now*."

He stepped right into my face. "Okay, I take it back."

"I'm nothing like my sister, okay? What I say to you I mean. When I do something with you it's because I feel..." I stopped, wasn't sure if I was making any sense. Or maybe I wasn't sure if I should finish the sentence.

"Because you feel what?"

"You know what."

"And I've had that feeling, too, for a long time now."

"You mean..." I gazed into his chocolate brown eyes, looking for the truth in them. His face leaned toward mine then my head titled and leaned toward his. Our lips met, a light feathery brush, then as our arms wrapped around one another, an insistent, deep pressing.

As our tongues slipped into one another's mouths, in the back of my head I wondered if there was a way to convince him to have anal sex with me.

***

Two years ago, the weekend after dinner...

Gabriel walked ahead of us, as we closed on the wolf exhibit at the Metroparks Zoo. Johanna speed walked up to him, and they started talking while Bobby and me lingered at the bars.

Bobby canted his head for a second toward Gabriel. "What's up with him?"

"We had a fight last night."

His eyebrow rose. "You two got into a fight? Well, you're practically married, so I shouldn't be surprised. What about?"

"I'd rather not say."

Both of his eyebrows rose. "Aren't you always the one telling Johanna she should be more open with me?"

I glanced over at Johanna in the distance, saw her standing there staring open mouth at me. "Looks like Gabriel just told her." I sighed. "Guess you'll know by tonight. Come on, we better catch up with them."

"Why am I always the last one to know?" Bobby called out, as I headed toward the wolf exhibit.

When we reached them, Bobby hooked a thumb into a belt loop of Johanna's shorts. I stood next to Bobby, letting he and Johanna be a buffer between Gabriel and me. One of the wolves sniffed another wolf's butt, and Bobby's hand discretely slipped to cup Johanna's ass.

"You can forget about ever putting your dick there," Johanna said then walked off, as Gabriel kept pace with her.

I nudged Bobby with an elbow. "Look who's fighting now."

***

Maybe my mistake with Gabriel was letting him choose, I thought, as Bobby's and mine's tongues danced with one another. I pushed Bobby away. "You want me, don't you?"

His eyes pleaded me. "For a longtime now, Candace."

"Then get on your knees and prove it."

Bobby did as told, and I shoved my crotch into his face. He unbuckled my shorts and pulled them down. Next this finger hooked into the hem of my panties, and a moment later they joined my shorts on the floor. My patch stood before him.

He eyed it for a moment, as if to get a lay of the land, then his tongue licked my inner thighs, each lap getting closer to my pum-pum until at last he ran it up and down my cleft, slowly separating it. My eyes closed, as I let go little gasps.

And then his warm mouth pulled gently at my lips, exposing my clit. His tongue moved to it, first treating it to broad, gentle swaths, then honing in on it with its tip in clockwise circles.

As I caressed his the crown of his head, his tongue went fully around my clit, over and over. I murmured in pleasure, nipples hardening, as he almost imperceptibly increased the speed of his licks.

My legs weakened, and a pulse of pleasure filled my lap. I grabbed a shock of his hair. Pulling his head away from my pum-pum, I looked him straight in the eyes. "Do you want to fuck me? Uh, big boy, do you want to fuck me?"

Smiling, he nodded eagerly.

"Well then, first you've got to do me a favor."

His eyebrows rose.

"I have something that I think you'll be *up* for. But I'm telling you right now – if you're not interested in doing it, we have no future together. Got it?"

His brown furrowed, then he slowly nodded.

"Excellent. Now get your clothes off and go into the bedroom. From this moment on, you will do exactly as I say."

***

One month ago...

Bobby caressed my shoulder and arm as I cried, yet again. A whiskey neat gal like me shouldn't being crying after a breakup, especially since it was eighteen months ago.

"I'm just so lonely," I got out between sobs.

"It's okay to feel that way," Bobby says. "I understand."

My mother had stopped comforting me a month after the breakup, told me to move on. Johanna didn't even give me a day, just said to quit being a crybaby, the same old thing she'd said to me while we were teenagers.

"You have no one to blame for this but yourself," she said. "I *told* you not to say anything."

Only Bobby showed any sympathy. And though I'd always found him attractive, thanks to his kindness, with each day I only fell deeper in love with him.

Maybe one day Johanna and I might patch things up; she was my sister after all. But a relationship with Bobby? Unrequited love never would work out.

I dabbed my eyes with the tissue Bobby handed me and tried to pull myself together. I needed to get way. *Far away.*

Alyssia, my friend from Tri-C days, told me there were jobs in Nashville. Yes, that's where I would go, I thought. I'll call her, see if I can stay a few days, and look for a job there.

Nashville will be my next chapter.

***

I placed two pillows under my lower tummy, lifting my butt, then spread my legs wide. "Lick my ass," I ordered. "And I don't mean my cheeks – I mean my asshole."

Bobby didn't have to be asked twice. He got on his knees behind me. A second later, his tongue, warm and moist, slid around the rim of my ass.

"Mhmmm," escaped my lips, as my eyes closed.

Then Bobby kissed where he licked, and I moaned then sighed in pleasure. He repeated the rim with his tongue than spiraled in on my netherhole.

The tip of his tongue dipped into my ass. My moans rose in volume, as my pussy grew wet

My pussy wasn't where I wanted his cock though.

I involuntarily bucked, trying to grind against his face, to get his tongue to go deeper. His large hands cupped my ass cheeks, separating them, and his breath ran hot against my butt as his tongue returned to rimming.

Then it dived back into my ass until his lips touch my butt cheeks. My breathing fell ragged.

He stood and squeezed onto my crack the lube I'd gotten him. His finger dipped into the river of gel. "My turn to surprise you."

Oh my, is this really happening? "You're going to put your finger in me?" I said hesitantly, afraid if I said it, he'd pull a Gabriel. "Then your...penis?"

"Yes. Once you are comfortable with it, it's really rewarding."

Thank you, God! "I know."

Bobby didn't say anything for a moment, and I looked over my shoulder at me. His eyebrows rose. "You've done this before?" he said.

"No. But I've read about it. Watched a lot of videos about it. Fantasized a lot about it too. Have *you* done it before?"

"Rimming – yes. Fingering – yes. Penetration – no."

"With Johanna?"

He laughed. "That prude?"

I grinned. "Yeah, what was I thinking?"

"Well, after tonight, you'll no longer be an anal virgin."

I turned my face back to the mattress, gripped the sheets tighter. "Then let's go all the way."

***

Bobby slowly pressed his finger into my netherhole. A surprise sensation of pressure filled me, yet also a slight thrumming spread through my body, as I let go an "Oooh." My senses heightened, his bright, citrus fragrance filled my nostrils, and his finger squeaked as it slid just a little deeper.

He slowly pressed further with each stroke, fell into a steady rhythm. An "Ahh" escaped my lips each time he pushed. The thrumming inside me grew, as if an acoustic guitar had been joined by another instrument for a richer, fuller feeling.

Then when he was knuckle deep, his finger began thrusting in and out of my ass. I murmured in pleasure, as the lube, like pond ripples, spread all over my ass and on my thighs, each time he did to me what no other man had.

A slow burning heat built inside of me. I wanted him deeper in me, all the way in me, even if it was just his finger. My head fell to the mattress as my hands reached back, grabbed each ass cheek, and spread them apart for him.

23

Bobby's middle finger went in to the second knuckle, then he slipped another finger fully into my vagina, began fucking both holes at once.

Whimpering, I ran a hand under my tummy, found my clit. The thrumming turned to fast-paced pulses, a full concert of sensations through my body.

As I circled my clit, his finger in my pussy abandoned it and joined its companion at my netherhole. He pressed, and a moment later, two of his fingers thrust hard and deep in my ass.

My moaning and gasping rose in volume, as every muscle in me tightened. My hand moved back to holding both cheeks apart for him, and my hips rocked against his finger.

I might just cum without even needing to touch my clit.

***

With fingers still buried in my ass, Bobby pulled my hips up so that I was on my knees. Then he withdrew himself, got on his own knees behind me.

A little nervous about the pain factor, I trembled. Two fingers were one thing, but a cock? Despite all I'd heard, my body tensed in fear.

He pressed his dick against my netherhole, and his spongy head easily slipped in with the hole his fingers had created. Then as the hard portion of his dick pressed in, my sphincter muscle tightened.

Bobby kept pushing forward, though, and after a few millimeters – though to me it felt like yards – he'd paused and let me get used to it. I took shallow breaths until comfortable. By the time a third of his dick was in me, my sphincter muscle relaxed and loosened. That's when it hit me. Every nerve in my body pulsed, as if it were consumed by the music and laser beams of the greatest rock show I'd ever seen.

And then, before I knew it, he was half-way in. Every part of my body wanted to cheer, to scream, and I heard nothing but a pulsing pleasure.

"Oh my God," I got out between gasps, "it's so big."

Gasping, I grabbed the sheets even harder, as my nails dug into the mattress. *Somehow he's indirectly stimulating my clitoris...maybe touching the shared sensory nerves.* But any ability to reason vanished as pleasure coursed through each cell in me, like I were high, as if it were transcendent.

A few strokes later, his full length was inside me, and his pace picked up.

My neck arched, as both eyes rolled to the back of my head. "Fuck," I got out between gasps, "...it's so deep."

That only encouraged him to go faster. His thighs slapped my cheeks, echoing across the walls, as he pounded into my ass, fucking it – fucking me – like he was a crazed animal. I could barely catch my breath, and as I shouted "Oooooh!" it vibrated to his thrusts. Every
muscle in my body tightened.

He made one last slam, and growled as his warm cum filled my ass. In the same instant, my body spasmed, and my head flew back, as I screamed "Fuck!" My body convulsed, seemingly forever, in utter silence. Then...a sense of total peace overcame me.

***

In the quiet afterglow, each of us wrapped in sheets and sweaty limbs, we gazed upon one another with amazement, then burst into laughter. It felt freeing to laugh after such an intense orgasm, as if my years of waiting for it, for that night's moments of enjoyment and shared pleasure with Bobby could be openly celebrated.

"That was…so good," I said, still dizzy.

"That…was…intense," he said between breaths.

"That was…profound."

He wrapped an arm around me, and I nuzzled my cheek against his chest. "Your ass is so small and tight, every nerve in my cock was on fire."

"You touched me in places that I never thought could be stimulated." I laughed again, reveling at our freedom, then turned my head to look at him. Reality set in. "This complicates things doesn't it?"

He canted his head so that our eyes met. "If this is what intimacy between us is like, then I don't want to lose you."

I knew talking about marriage was getting ahead of myself. But this time I was on the right road and was going to keep driving. After all, it was Bobby.

Atonement

My phone beeped, indicating a new text. I picked it up from the hotel bedspread and hoped it was him. I'd had the itch all through the conference, and the Luxe Oasis' streaming options weren't cutting it.

I'm here, the text read.

Barefoot, I traipsed across the carpeted floor and opened the door. A man – short-cropped black hair atop a sharp face sporting a straight, commanding nose and determined lips – stood there. His mysterious brown eyes stared at me. He smelled of amber and vetiver, while his navy blue blazer with white tee and ecru slacks left no doubt this his body was muscular and sturdy, like a raging bull.

"Clara?" he said.

I nodded.

"Jaquan." That wasn't his real name, I was certain of it. Escorts never used their real names.

He pressed past me, entering the room, looked nonchalantly at the décor. "Let's get going."

I closed the door and went for my slip-ons.

Jaquan looked me up and down. "That's what you're wearing?"

"Is there something wro–"

"We're in Vegas. Dress glitzy."

I let out a slight laugh. "My, you are demanding."

His expression remained hard. "You read my profile, correct?"

"Yes."

"And that's what you wanted?"

"Yes."

"Then why are you surprised?"

I stared at his face for a moment. "It's more delight than surprise."

He didn't break my gaze for a long moment, as if trying to determine whether or not I was telling the truth. At last, he seemed to be satisfied that I was. "Keep your delight to yourself. The way you express it is insulting and unbecoming of you."

I lowered my head and just stood there, like my secretary in Denver did when she couldn't think of what to say after I'd berated her. Finally, I responded, "Yes sir."

"Let me guess. You didn't bring anything glitzy."

"Well, it's a business conference–"

"A business conference *in Vegas*." He picked up the room phone's receiver and held it out to me, as he punched a couple of numbers. "Order a dress from the hotel store."

"What?" I took the receiver.

"Tell them you want the green short hoco dress. The one with the V-neck, V-back, and sequins. And don't forget the high heels."

I gave them my size. The cost was several hundred dollars, but they'd have it delivered to my room in a few minutes. I wondered if he was getting some kickback from the hotel store.

After hanging up, we stood there for a moment in silence.

"Tell me about yourself," he said.

"I'm the vice president of employee productivity at Grayer Corp. in Houston. Originally I'm from–"

"Stop," he said. "I don't care about that."

"You just ask–"

"I didn't come here to argue about what *I* said. I know what *I* said. You apparently don't."

He's kind of an asshole, I thought, but his toned body and large hands made my spine tingle, so I gave him a mulligan.

There was a knock at the door.

I went to it, and a bellboy stood in the hallway holding my new dress in a plastic bag and the high heels in a box. "Dress delivery for Clara?"

"That's me." I tipped him then took my clothes toward the bathroom.

"Where are you going?" Jaquan said.

"To put this on."

"Do it out here. Christ, I'm going to see you naked later tonight. You might as well give me a good look at what to expect."

I brought the clothes to the bed and undressed. Jaquan watched me the entire time, as if I were just a plaything for his pleasure. He didn't give any indication if he liked what he saw, but I supposed that didn't matter since I'd paid him.

When I pulled the dress out of the bag, I had to admit it was beautiful, though maybe more something a young woman rather than a middle-aged business exec would don. Its corset bodice of dazzling emerald beads and sequins created a striped pattern that drew the eyes to my barely contained breasts. The skirt extended to mid-thigh, and the spaghetti straps over the shoulder formed a V-shaped open back. The dress left as much of my body exposed as it covered. The matching high heels lifted the back of my feet an inch off the floor, jutting out my ass.

Jaquan grinned for the first time since he'd been there. "Very nice." He walked toward the door.

I grabbed my purse and followed. "For dinner, I was thinking The Oliv–"

"We're going to The Viola."

I gulped. Everyone at the conference had warned me about how overpriced it was.

"You make plenty of money, you can afford it," Jaquan said, as if reading my mind.

We entered the elevator.

"May I ask you a question?" I said.

He looked at me side-eyed. The elevator came to a stop. "Yeah, *a* question, during dinner." He grabbed hold of my hand – his seemed to swallow mine – just as the elevator doors swished open, and we entered the casino. Men not engrossed in their games stared, as I walked past.

On the far side of the casino was The Viola. Another kickback? As we reached the maître d, Jaquan let go of my hand. I missed the warmth of his large palm and fingers.

"Jaquan and Clara, special reservations," my escort said.

The maître d grabbed two menus. "Right this way, sir."

Men at their dinner tables snuck glances of my legs, as we passed until finally ending up at a dark corner in the back.

"A bottle of the cabernet sauvignon," Jaquan said to the maître d. When he'd left, my escort turned to me. "What was your question?"

"Back in the room, you asked me to tell you about myself. What did you really mean?"

He sat back, took his time to answer. "I don't care where you work or where you come from. That's superficial. What I want to know is *why* you called me. That's the real you."

"Does that mat–"

He held his hand up. "You said *question*. It wasn't plural."

I bowed my head again, just as my regional manager had when I told him his building's productivity was too low and he better get it taken care of or he wouldn't be taking any more rides up the elevator to his office. And then I laid out exactly what I expected him to do.

Jaquan and I remained silent as looking over the menu. A waiter arrived and poured a dollop of wine into Jaquan's glass to sample, waited for his approval, then filled both of our glasses. "Are you ready to order?" the waiter said.

"I'll have the prime ribeye 18 oz., and the lady will have the prime filet mignon 9 oz."

"Very good sir. I'll have the salads right out."

The Viola didn't list its prices on the menus; I guess if you had to ask, you couldn't afford it. I figured dinner was already up to $250 though.

"You're not going to let me ask my question are you?" I said.

"You wouldn't want me to."

He was right, I wouldn't.

I tried to think of something to say but was out of my realm. The uncomfortableness felt...good. "Thank you for selecting this restaurant." I said. "It is much nicer than The Olive."

He nodded. "That's much better. Appreciation looks good on you."

I smiled and stayed quiet, uncertain if I should thank him. No, best to keep complimenting his power, I decided. That's what last spring's intern in my office always did to me, and he got a terrific reference.

"The dress looks good on you," he said before I could think of something to say. "I like the way the men stared jealously when you walked past."

I nodded. "You were right. This is much better than what I had planned to wear."

He leaned back again, gazed at me as if assessing the intention of my words. "If you are saying any of this because you hope to gain favor with me, you can stop. I plan to do what I please with you, whether you approve or not."

As you should, I thought, that's what I hired you for.

The waiter brought our salads, mixed greens with champagne vinaigrette.

A few bites into it, he pulled the glass plate away from me. "Don't you think you've had enough?"

I looked up, as my jaw dropped.

"You have your weight to watch after all."

I bowed my head again. Damn, he was good. "Of course. You are right."

When the waiter stopped to refill our water, Jaquan had him take my plate away.

At last, the prime rib arrived. He dug right in.

"This is very good," I said after taking a bite. "Thank you for ordering it for me."

Jaquan nodded. His strong jawline, set as if it had been chiseled from stone, had me staring at him. Then he set down his fork and knife and stared right back at me. "You still haven't told me who the *real* you is."

I cut a small piece of the prime filet mignon as trying to think of an answer. "I still don't understand the question."

"I think you do. You're not stupid. Or maybe you are, given that you didn't pack a decent dress for Vegas."

My head drooped again, and I cut more slowly.

"Why does a woman like you want to be humiliated?" he said.

"Humiliation isn't what I'm seeking."

"When *you* control someone, you humiliate them, either deliberately to maintain power or because you take some sick pleasure in doing so."

"Are you my shrink now?"

He sneered. "I need to know to ensure I...don't go *too far* later."

"You have been doing well up to now."

"Got your panties wet already, do I?"

I blushed. "No."

"Good. Your dress is shear enough that a wet spot would show. You've already embarrassed yourself enough tonight."

I almost shed a tear at that. "If I tell you–"

"If you tell me what?"

"Will you..." I wasn't sure how to say it. "Will you...keep humiliating me?"

He nodded. "I may even turn it up a notch."

My pussy tingled at that, but I still wasn't sure how to start.

"Let me guess," he said with a half-growl, as if tired of waiting for me. "All of your life, you've gotten your way – daddy's little girl, teacher's pet..."

He was right. "As a young woman, guys kneeled before me

because I was out of their league while employees and mid-level managers jumped exactly how high I told them to because they feared losing their jobs." I looked up. "But it was a trap."

He nodded then his eyes canted toward my steak. "Don't eat too much more of that. Your *weight*."

I suddenly felt hollow inside but continued. "No one treated me out of respect. Oh, they were respectful and polite, but it all was fake, driven by a desire to climb the social ladder through me or in fear of being knocked down a couple of rungs."

He grinned, took another bite of his prime ribeye, chewed it leisurely. "Go on."

"And so they were tenderfooted, always quick to correct their course if they perceived that they weren't somehow pleasing me. The worse were the men in bed, who always let me make the first move, and the second, and the third, never surprising or delighting me, who satisfied me only because I told them how to do so. How...well, unsatisfying."

He chuckled at that. "You dumb fucking cunt."

My eyes glowered at him. *Here I am, opening myself up to him, and he's insulting me.* And yet, with each dig, somehow I felt...cleaner. "Goddamn it, if I want it, I deserve it. I've put the work in. I've learned to charm, I've studied my ass off, I've worked out relentlessly to stay in shape, I've spent hours every day analyzing the numbers. I've earned it."

A shit-eating grin covered his face. "What did you earn, princess?"

"I've earned the right to *not* be treated like a princess. I've earned the right to be fucked the way I wanted to be fucked."

"And how do you want to be fucked?"

Roughly and without apology. But I didn't say it.

34

He went back to cutting his prime ribeye. "That's all right, you don't have to say it. I know what you want. But I'm going to order desert first."

I crossed my arms, as my upper lip curled. First he'd tried to break me, I thought, now he's trying to piss me off. Actually, he did a fairly good job on both counts. Regardless, angry, humiliated, confused, I couldn't eat.

When the waiter came to clear our plates, Jaquan ordered the crème brulée.

The waiter looked at me. "And you, ma'am?"

"The lady isn't having desert," Jaquan said. "She's watching her waistline."

A shocked look covered the young man's face. "Very well," he said, and hurried off to the kitchen.

I decided to salvage the evening. "Where will we go after dinner?"

"To your room, of course."

My eyes widened. "We're not going to a show?"

"Have you ever been outside in Vegas during July? If we walk in this heat, you'll look disheveled by the time we get back to the room. I don't want my enjoyment to be diminished because I'm with a slob."

"I could freshen up when we get back, before we...you know."

He shook his head slowly, dismissively. "Show tickets run $100 in Vegas. You've already spent enough money tonight, haven't you?"

"This is *my* evening of pleasure," I said.

"And your pleasure is *my* business."

I wondered how many times I'd said to mid-level and

regional managers exactly what he'd just said to me.

The waiter brought the crème brulée. As he ate, I sat silently, hungry but unable to eat even if there had been food in front of me. Was it my anger at him or my anticipation of what was to come that churned my stomach?

When Jaquan finished, he rose and held out his hand to me. "Come, my little flower. Time to get plucked." As we walked the length of the restaurant and the casino to the elevator, men with lustful eyes stared at my legs and ass.

Once in the room, he said, "I suspect you know the routine."

I went to my purse and placed a $50 bill for the tip on the nightstand. I'd already prepaid with the credit card when I ordered online.

He stared at the bill and sighed. "You'll be putting another fifty on the nightstand when I'm done with you."

My eyes tightened.

"I've already laid out on online what I offer, and you've set out what you'd like to happen when soliciting me. Have those terms changed at all?"

I shook my head.

"Then the negotiation is done." He went to the bathroom, turned on the sink tap, and walked out with a partially wet towel. Plopping himself onto the bed, he leaned up against the headboard. "Strip for me, you dirty slut."

I kicked off my heels and started swaying side to side. Turning around, my eyes looked over my shoulder at him, as I shook my butt. Then swirling back toward him, I ran my hands through my hair.

He sat there still, watching. ""Move slower."

I decreased my speed, pulled the spaghetti strips down my

arms and off them. As I did, my top fell forward. I bent forward, shook my bare breasts.

Shimmying the dress over my hips, I let it fall below me. With just my panties on, I pulled them off one leg at a time.

Before I could finish my second leg, though, Jaquan was off the bed, marching toward me. "No, no, not like that. Put those panties back on."

My eyebrows furrowed, as I pulled my undergarment up.

"Here's how you do it," Jaquan said. He hooked his finger into the side of my panties then withdrew it. "Now do the same, both sides."

He watched my hands, making sure they were in the right spot. "Turn around."

I did.

"Now *slowly* roll them down your thigh, shaking your ass as you do. When they reach beneath your thigh, let go, so they fall to the floor. Then step out of them as shimmying."

Just like I'd micromanaged one regional sales director.

I did as he asked, and he grinned. "Better." He went back to the bed. "Continue."

Continue? I was naked. Still, I gave him a show. I shook my bare breasts. I twirled around slowly, shaking my hips. My hands went to my ass cheeks, caressing them. Then I pivoted back toward him, ran my hands over my breasts then down my hips swaying back and forth.

I stole glances at his cock rising through his pants.

Cupping my breasts, I squeezed them together then tossed my head back, as if he were pleasuring me. Facing him, I placed a finger in my mouth, sucked on it long and slow, suggesting what I might do if it were his cock.

Jaquan grimaced. "I've seen better. Good thing you don't have to work on the streets for your money or you'd starve." He rose from the bed, took out a tiny bottle from the inside pocket of his blazer then slipped that off as well. "Lay on the bed, on your tummy. Get comfortable." He chuckled.

From the bed, I watched him. He took his time undressing, folding each item of his clothing and ensuring it was set out neatly on the room's desk. His nude body was smooth, sculpted, masculine...in short, magnificent.

Jaquan tossed the tiny bottle on the nightstand and to the bed, where it landed next to my thighs. Crawling onto the mattress, he hovered over me, kissing along my shoulder to the neck. I let go a soft moan, as the tightness in my muscles evaporated. When he leaned in to kiss up my neck, his cock grazed my thigh. His large hand caressed my hair, and then he wrapped a shock of it around his fist and pulled my head off the mattress. I gasped. His teeth bit into my neck, and I squealed.

"You fucking bitch, I know what you want."

His free hand slowly traced down the length of my side over the back of a thigh and shoved itself between the mattress and my pussy, where he found me wet.

He chuckled. "I told you I knew."

Jaquan let go off my hair then straddled my legs above the knees. His hands caressed my ass cheeks, squeezed each one, then pulled them apart so my netherhole was entirely exposed to him.

"You are such a loathsome bitch, that I'm going to do something for you that I bet no other guy ever has. I'm going to stimulate your A-spot until you cum."

38

A-spot?

"And when you cum, it'll be like nothing you've ever experienced before. When I'm done with you, you'll forget about all those guys whose small dicks you dirtied with your cunt."

The cap for his tiny bottle popped open, and a glob of something went onto his hands, which he rubbed together.

"Grab your ass cheeks and spread them."

I took a check in each hand and held them apart for him.

He spat on my ass, perfectly hitting my netherhole. His warm spit pooled there, then his hands massaged the crevasse between my cheeks, and once wet with the lube he'd squirted onto his hands, his fingers took over, rubbing the rim around my hole.

The tip of his pinkie pressed against it, and I jerked.

Jaquan moved off my legs to a side. His knees settled next to my ribs, then his hand went to the back of neck and grabbed it, holding me in place, as his other hand returned to my hole.

His pinkie pushed against it, and though I squirmed, the fear of his vice like-grip on the back of my neck forced me to control myself.

Once his pinkie was in, he slowly rocked it back and forth until it was knuckle deep. My eyes closed, as I bit my lower lip. Juices from my pussy wetted the bedsheet below me.

I moaned.

"You see, I'm in control now, princess," he said as thrusting his pinkie deeper into me.

And his dominance was mine to enjoy.

Once he got his pinkie in as far as it would go, he withdrew it. Relief overcame me, like when the nurse stops tightening the blood pressure cuff on your arm.

Then he did something with the lube bottle and pressed his thicker, longer middle finger into my ass.

My eyes flew open, as I gasped.

He'd so loosened the muscles at my netherhole that they barely squeezed against his finger, as he pushed it deeper inside me, stopping only when the knuckles of those fingers folded against his palm met my ass cheeks. Then he thrust it deeper still, so the knuckles dug into my ass's soft flesh, and paused.

And then he pressed not further in but downward so his finger touched the wall of my vagina, right near my cervix.

A sudden, funny feeling overcame me, like that moment when you're on the top of the roller coaster and about to go down.

Then that sensation seamlessly transformed into something entirely else, one of immense pleasure emanating from the very center of my body. Heat flooded my stomach, and for a moment it felt like the contentment of holding your face toward the sun to warm it.

His free hand slid under my pussy, and inserting a finger into it, he quickly found my clit among the wet mess. Pleasure thrummed through every cell in my body.

Wetness filled my pussy, and I wondered at first if I'd pissed the bed, but it was merely vaginal lubrication that my body somehow was secreting in copious amounts. I'd never had anyone rub my clit lead to me releasing this much lubricant and pleasure. It had to be because he was applying pressure to that one spot. If that was it – just applying pressure, not flicking it or rubbing it or anything else – I never wanted him to stop pressing there.

And then a profound, molten-hot sensation that made me want to yell, "Right there! Don't stop!" overcame me, and I moaned louder than I'd ever had before. Every muscle in my body tensed, tighter than ever before, and released so I found myself reduced to a puddle of flesh. For an instant, I loved him more than anyone else in the entire world and unconditionally, as joyful tears streamed down my cheeks. He was right, that was the best orgasm of my life.

Jaquan did nothing for a moment, just let my body calm down, then he slowly pulled his fingers out of my vagina and ass, leaving me feeling empty, as if the love of my life went in an instant from warmly kissing me to a thousand miles away.

He got behind me, his knees on both sides of my thighs, then gripped my legs and pushed them under me so my ass stuck higher in the air. My thighs remained close together. I was soft clay for him to mold as he pleased.

He lifted my right leg up and pushed his own folded leg under it. His cock pressed against my pussy lips and slid in me; he didn't use any lube, didn't need to, for I already was sopping wet.

"In the *Kama Sutra*," he said, "this is called the elephant position. I thought it an appropriate position for fucking you, given how you have to watch your weight."

His hand took a fistful of my hair and pulled, holding my head up so I was looking at the headboard as his cock pummeled me, each time touching that same spot deep inside that his finger had pressed. My mouth opened, moaning with each of his thrusts.

"Tilt your tush higher, princess," he said.

I did, and the pleasure increased. My breathing quickened. "Oh fuck," I moaned.

He fucked me harder, his punishing thrusts animalistic, primitive. Penetration had never felt so good, as my escort kept plunging deep inside me, deeper than anyone had before, deeper than I imagined was possible.

This control freak got to be controlled.

And then with one last thrust, he froze as he growled, and his cum spurt inside me. My body tensed again, then I spasmed and screamed in pleasure. For the longest moment, my body seemed to float in warm water, utterly satisfied and at peace.

Then, after a moment, he rolled off me and lay on the bed, a sheen of sweat across his muscular body. "And what about that tip?" he said.

With knees of rubber, I walked naked over to my purse, and dug out another fifty for him.

He laughed. "You're a cheapskate, aren't you? Guess that's how you got rich."

I pulled out another hundred.

"Finally, some appreciation."

I came back to the bed, but as reaching for him he stood and wiped his fingers with the wet towel, then went to his clothes.

"That should keep you for a while," he said as pulling up his boxers, "a little atonement for fucking so many others in the ass. Metaphorically of course."

I crossed my legs, hiding most of my pussy from him. His cum had started to drip from it.

"Well?" he said sharply. "Do you need more?"

I folded my arms over my breasts. "No."

He shook his head. "Guess you're going back to being a cunt

now."

I watched him finish dressing, and when he flexed his shoulders so the suit jacket fell perfectly upon him, he picked up the $200 on the nightstand and smiled.

"It's been a pleasure, ma'am," he said. "Enjoy your stay in Las Vegas."

With that, he walked out of the room, softly closing the door behind him.

The room was quiet, but the flashing casino signs and the stream of traffic headlights suggested all was otherwise on the Strip below.

My phone beeped. I picked it up from the nightstand. A text from Howard Reynolds, our regional director in Boise, responding to my phone call from earlier that day.

I didn't read it, simply typed back: *Your staff's error count is far too high. I'm flying in Wednesday to clean up your fucking mess.*

I hit SEND and grinned.

Dangerous Man (A Heart Play)

He sat down on the barstool next to me like we were old friends. I glanced at him; with his sandy blond hair, he looked younger than the crow's feet suggested, but what most drew me were his eyes – gray, like slate with an azure tinge, rare and mysterious.

When I reached the end of my Negroni, he tapped my wrist. "Can I buy you another?"

"Good thing I'm not an English teacher, or I'd say something snarky like 'I don't know, *can* you?'"

"I'm glad you aren't," he grinned, "or I'd have to back away, foiled by your pedantry."

I giggled. "Good answer. Yes, you may."

He signaled the bartender to refill both of our drinks then turned to me. "I'm Noel."

"Simone."

His eyebrow rose. "Simone. A sultry name."

"I'm a passionate woman, Noel. Do you like passionate women?"

"I like women in any flavor they come. And I like what I see on the menu now."

I laughed. "My, my, you are forward."

He shrugged. "When I see what I like, I go for it."

"But do you *take* it? Are you a dangerous man, Noel?"

"What if I am...*dangerous*?"

I laughed again. "*Noel* hardly sounds like a dangerous man's name."

"It's part of my mild-mannered persona."

"It's a brilliant disguise."

The bartender brought us our drinks. His amber poison looked to be a bourbon.

Noel took a sip, then as we gazed at one another, he said, "You have the most beautiful blue turquoise eyes I've ever seen."

"Does that sound like a something a dangerous man would say?"

Noel didn't seemed fazed. "In truth, I think I should be afraid of *you*."

"Me? Why me?" I drank from my glass. The Campari's strong bitter note gave way to the vermouth's sweetness.

"With eyes like those, you could easily wrap a man around your little finger."

"Even a dangerous man like you?"

"It's eyes like yours that make me dangerous."

"How's that?"

"The more you assert yourself, in any way, the more likely I will make a bold countermove by asserting myself. Things can quickly spin out of control."

"You make it sound like international politics." I took another sip, this time caught more of the gin's herbal flavor.

"I just want to be up front, to be...*honest*."

"To be honest, I've had enough to drink. Want to get out of here?"

"I have a very nice room at the Paso Del Norte."

For a moment I examined his face, as if to see whether or not he was truly dangerous. "All right," I said. "Lead the way. But first, you pay for our drinks – and don't forget the one I had before you arrived."

***

Arm in arm, we stepped into the warm El Paso night, the lights of the county courthouse reflecting off the asphalt. We walked the four blocks in silence, not asking about where the other worked, if we were married or in a relationship, if we lived in El Chuco or were just visiting. We didn't need to ask such questions.

The moment Noel opened the door to his suite, I was impressed. A living area was separate from the bedroom, all of it spacious and lit by the soft August moonlight. Two stems of cream-colored freesia rose from a clear glass vase on the coffee table. Noel closed the door and then came the click and slide of the chain lock. He took hold of my arm and faced me.

His lips met mine. Hard. Passionately. We moved our hands all over each other's faces and through each other's hair and kept kissing, deeply. I wrapped my legs around Noel, and he picked me up by the underside of my thighs, backed me against the wall, and we stayed in that position as kissing.

Mhm, he wants to get right to it. Fine by me.

His tongue parted my lips and slipped into my mouth, as his hand slid up the length of my thigh and waist. His erection pressed against the cleft between my legs, and I rubbed up and down it. Our mouths parted, and I tried to catch my breath. *Yeah,* I told myself, *that was bourbon in his glass back at the bar.*

Then his hands slipped under my blouse and reaching

behind my back, unsnapped my bra

His fingers glided along my skin back to my waist and lifted the blouse over my breasts. He yanked the bra below them then cupped one as his tongue went to my nipple, flicking it over and over. My neck arched and eyes closed, moaning in pleasure as the nipple hardened. Then his warm mouth fell on to it, pinching it with his lips and sucking on it. My clit twitched.

A moment later, he shifted to my other breast, sucking its nipple, as his hands pulled the blouse over my head and the bra straps down my shoulders. He lowered me to my feet so I was standing – I missed his hardness pressed against my cleft – and he unbuttoned my skirt. Pulling down the skirt and the panties underneath, they fell to the carpet, as his warm mouth kissed my tummy. I stepped out of my shoes and the fallen garments while he sucked again on a breast, and I found the simple task so difficult for my head spun with dizziness from his ministrations.

He moved back, and naked I filled the space then undid his tie. "You don't waste any time, do you, Noel?" As I unbuttoned his shirt, my fingers paused to play with his chest hair. A woodsy scent with a slight hint of citrus to it rose from his exposed body.

Noel's hands cupped my breast, caressing and squeezing them, as I undid his belt then stroked his cock through his dress pants. His breathing deepened, and my fingers carefully unzipped then tugged down the pants and his boxers. His cock bobbed outward, tapping my tummy, while gravity did the rest of the work undressing him. He lightly pinched my nipple then let go to take off his shirt, as his feet slipped out of his shoes and somehow managed to remove his socks, all while I gently grazed his abs with my fingernails.

Once he was nude, I stepped back, admiring his body. "You don't *seem* dangerous, Noel."

His gray eyes narrowed. "Get on your knees."

I squatted then shifted my weight so my knees pressed into the carpet, my face level with the base of his cock. Apparently this wasn't fast enough for him, as his large hand went to the crown of my head and pushed my face forward onto his cock, which he held straight out with his other hand.

My lips quickly parted, but there was no time to play with this new toy, for he shoved it in, hitting my tonsils. I let out a grunt, but he didn't care. As his hand held my head in place, he slowly thrust his cock in and out of me. I kept my mouth opened wide so I could breathe, then he tilted my head up so his cock would go into my throat. He lightly slapped my cheek, and my mouth involuntarily closed; fortunately I was able to wrap my teeth under my lips so I didn't bite him.

But then I needed to breathe and unable to tell him, I pressed my hands on his thighs, tried to push him away, but his other hand came to my head, and the speed of his hip thrusts grew faster. "Don't fight it, Simone," he said. "You need to get this cock good and wet for what we're going to do next."

His cock went even deeper into my throat until his balls slapped my chin, as he fucked my face. My fingernails dug into his thighs, trying to tell him that my lungs burned from no air, but whatever pain I inflicted didn't faze him, maybe even encouraged him.

At last he pulled out, my saliva forming a long arcing string between the head of his cock and my lips, and I fell back, trying to catch my breath.

I wanted to say "What the fuck, Noel?" but before I could he grabbed my arm and pulled me up then to the bed. He pushed me forward so I fell half on it, then he reached for something. A strap of cloth slid down my face and across my mouth. He pulled back on the cloth until it slid into my mouth, then he tied it tight on the back of my head.

"We can't have you bothering hotel security, now can we?" he said. "Those boys have more important things to do than to come knocking on our door."

Noel pulled my arms behind my back, and crossing my wrists, began tying them. I kicked, tried to scream through the cloth stuffed in my mouth, but then he grabbed a chunk of my hair and pulled me up to a standing position.

"Don't make me beat you," he hissed in my ear. "I will if I have to. Either way, we're going to do this tonight, so you might as well shut up and enjoy it."

He pressed my head into the mattress, bending me over. The coils of his rope cut into my wrists, as he finished tying it off.

"And if you don't like it, well, that's your fault, isn't it? You're the one who came here tonight. I told you I was a dangerous man. Now stay bent over the bed, and put that sexy ass in the air."

***

Noel cupped my ass cheeks, then his warm mouth kissed them then his hand squeezed, as I waited there, bent over the bed and tied up, frozen with uncertainty. Would he really hit me if I resisted?

There was a *click* of a cap then cold lube hit my ass crack. I shivered as it dripped over my netherhole and onto my pussy lips. *He will be rough,* I told myself, *steel yourself.* Two of his fingers slid back and forth through the lube then one pushed against my netherhole.

"No, not there!" I screamed, but with the cloth stuffed in my mouth it was just muffled words.

His fingertip pressed in, surprisingly gentle for a man having his way with me. Then there was a feeling of pressure as my sphincter tightened on him, but my body didn't tense. He didn't waste time, forced the finger all the way, and I wiggled.

Then, he inserted a second finger, pushing it forward until after just a couple of thrusts it was fully in as well.

His free hand pulled one ass cheek away, and he began to finger fuck my ass with abandon. My head spun, as if I were on a carnival ride, and a flush swept over me. *Damn it, what is wrong with me, I shouldn't be getting turned on by a man doing this to me.* Then my sphincter relaxed, as my own body betrayed me.

He sensed the lack of pressure on his fingers and removed them from my ass. Feeling the sudden emptiness, I resisted, pushing back, would not let my body beg for what he was doing to me. Then his hands parted my ass cheeks, and a gob of warm spit fell from his mouth into my netherhole. The tip of his erection came to it; his fingers had widened my sphincter hole enough that his spongy cockhead easily pressed into me.

The hardness of his erection, though, proved more difficult – his cock being much larger in diameter then his two fingers – but he was insistent. Soon he was in halfway, but that was more than enough for him, as his fucking of my ass began. My breasts shook like gelatin in rhythm to his thrusts, and I wished I could reach for them, could cup and squeeze them.

51

Then his hand grabbed the hair at the crown of my head, and pulled my head back so none of my upper body touched the mattress as he pounded into me. He leaned forward, his mouth almost to my ear, and hissed, "If you tell anyone about this, I'll kill you and your family."

Tears fell from my eyes onto my cheek, as my eyes winced.

Noel's thighs slapped mine as he had almost his entire cock in my ass. He pulled tighter on my hair, bringing my head back even farther.

"Oh, you were such a tease," he hissed. "But I told you I was a dangerous man."

My whole body tensed, and pleasure coursed through me, as if ripples on a pond.

Then came the full betrayal. My whole body spasmed, like every muscle in it were shocked with electricity, and I screamed through the mouth gag in a full body orgasm. I squirted from my pussy onto his thighs, as I spasmed again.

He slammed his cock one last time into me, growling, as his hot cum filled my ass.

***

After untying me, Noel caressed my ass with a warm washcloth until my muscles there relaxed. Then he held me close, soothing my hair. Once I'd regained my breath, he got up and with another washcloth cleaned his half-limp cock.

I rose as he did, but still dizzy and weak-kneed from the orgasm, I fell back on the bed. An ecstatic grin covered my fac. "Wow, two fantasies in one night."

"Two? We do anal all the time."

"Being tied up," I said.

"Ah. I counted that as part of the rape fantasy." He reclined on the bed next to me, grazed his finger along my curves. "You were sexy as hell."

"Thank you," I said then kissed him.

He chuckled, and his gray eyes caught a glint of moonlight. "Actually I should be thanking you."

"We should be thankful for each other. I never could do what we just did with anyone other someone I loved and trusted so much."

"Our life together is so precious."

"It is. And I'm glad you like passionate women."

"Well, I am a dangerous man – at least for tonight."

Partners

The man spoke in a low voice to me. "He's going to try scaring you. He gets off on that. Don't worry – he won't hurt you, unless you piss him off."

As the car door opened, he placed his hand on the top of my head to keep me from bumping the frame, while the other hand guided me out. We stood there for a long moment, then the man who spoke to me undid the ties on the blindfold.

I blinked back the light but in the dimness quickly regained my sight. A mansion, it backlit in the orange glow of a setting sun, rose before me. Waves lapped at a shoreline behind the massive, brick structure. A stocky man with an Uzi guarded the front door. *I guess there's no escape for the moment.*

The man who'd driven me there gripped my arm above the elbow, walked us to Uzi guy. "This is her," my kidnapper said. They nodded at one another, and we entered the mansion.

A chandelier larger than my bathtub hung above the expansive foyer. Thick, heavy wood and marble appeared to be his decorating style.

Then a black-suited, white-gloved butler stepped before us. "The Boss will see you now." He turned, and light glinted off the black earpiece he wore. His suit bulged right where a gun holster would go.

My heels clacked against the tile floor, and my red dress

swished below my knees, while we followed him. At the end of the hallway, he opened the oak double doors.

From inside the room, a man with a Mexican accent said, "My friends, *bienvenido*! Come in, come in!"

The scent of expensive cigars, rich and savory like dark chocolate mixed with black pepper, hit me as I entered the room, it heavy on mahogany, from the bookcases to the long desk. A man with dark hair and eyes like black onyx sat behind it in a plush leather chair.

My kidnapper led me to the front of the desk. "Thank you, Boss."

The Boss's gaze turned to me. "My, my, what have you here, Griffin? Is this the Serena Jones you were telling me about?" He rose from his desk, walked up to me, delicately ran a finger over my cheek. I remained absolutely still. "I have half a mind to keep her as my personal...*cortesana*."

I gulped.

"Still, I suppose she is worth more to me for her skills than in the bedroom. Besides, I prefer to *break in* my partners." He gave a mocking, cruel laugh. "Miss Jones, you owe me. First you spied on my men. That alone warrants death. Then you kill one of my men. I suppose that is not much of a loss; if a woman of your small stature was able to overcome him, he couldn't have been worth much. Still, he was my man and my loss, and there must be consequences for it. And then there's the matter of the money you never paid back.

"Now, my associate tells me you are a software programmer for some big company here in beautiful San Diego. It just so happens that I am in need of a hacker. To pay off your debts, he will take you to a special place where you can prove your worth to me."

"But I don't know anything about hacking. I *write* code."

His voice dropped an octave. "If you can write code, you can identify a program's weaknesses and break in...reverse engineering, if you will."

"It's not at all the same thing."

He stood next to me, tilted his head so he was near my ear, then lowered his voice. "I sell many items that I do not consume. Since I know how to sell, I can determine what my customers want; I don't need to consume those items to understand how to sell. It's no different for you with your coding. Now, listen carefully, you little cunt. If you do not prove your worth, I will ensure you suffer so much that you'll wish I'd instead dissolved your body in acid. *Comprende?*"

My eyes widened. I nodded.

"*Excellente.*" The Boss walked to a bar against the wall and poured an amber drink into three shot glasses. He handed one to me then to my kidnapper, and taking the last one, raised it in the air. "Código 1530 14 Year Old Extra Añejo. Only 400 bottles were made. A toast to our new relationship."

The man and I raised our glasses. The Boss tossed his down, and the man and then me followed. *Tequila. Damn good tequila.*

"Now, I must attend to some other matters," the Boss said. "I shall check with you in a week."

My kidnapper nodded, then placing a hand on my lower back, guided me out of the office.

"That went well," he whispered to me, as we left the mansion.

"Well? I think he threatened to have me gang raped."

"But you *weren't* gang raped. So it went well indeed."

***

We drove for an hour or so, though where we went, I had no idea, for I was blindfolded before getting into the car. When Griffin – at least that's what the Boss called him – turned off the engine and removed the black strap covering my eyes, I saw we were at a large house in a swanky part of San Diego. While not as impressive as the Boss's, it was better than what I'd ever imagined myself living in.

He turned to me, spoke in a deep timbre. "I think you know by now that running would be stupid."

I nodded.

He gazed at me with those garnet green eyes for a long moment, at first I thought to determine if I was telling the truth, but then I shivered under his glare and realized he wanted to impress upon me that trying to flee would not turn out well.

Once he saw me shrink back, he opened his car door. "Follow me."

The house was classic hacienda style – white stucco walls, rustic wood accents, wrought-iron fixtures. I wondered if there was something there that I could use a weapon, maybe a poker or a tong for the fireplace.

"You live here?" I said.

"I do now. It's where the Boss told us to work. So long as we're profitable for him, he'll let us stay here."

The man led me to the living room with computers and flat screens set out on a desk facing a bay window that overlooked the city below and the ocean in the distance.

"This is where you'll work," he said.

"Look, I don't know anything about hacking. I can't do this."

"You better try. The Boss explained what awaits if you don't."

"Do you think stressing me out somehow is helpful?"

"You were a lot more positive back at the house."

"I was desperate. And you tricked me, used sex to lull me into a sense of complacency. How can I trust you now?"

"Tricked you? You seemed to enjoy it, as I recall. As for trust, you better learn to trust me. I'm the only one you've got in this world." He waved an arm at the computers. "Take a seat. Get started."

He plopped himself into an arm chair in the corner, a strand of his brown hair flopping, and stared at me as I sat.

"Now? It's nighttime."

"The Boss didn't hire you to work nine to five."

I looked at the array of tech on the desk. Three Raspberry Pi computers, each with its own flat screen, all networked together. Powerful processors, ample RAM, probably a dedicated graphics card for password cracking or running virtual machine. Then there was the WiFi Pineapple, HackRF One, Flipper Zero, USB Rubber Ducky, LAN Turtle, all very expensive ... Who the fuck am I working for? And what the hell is the real name of this man who kidnapped me after we made love?

A paper atop the keyboard gave me instructions on my assignment and sign-in information. I logged on, and the entire time Griffin watched me from his chair. A heat rose in my belly, as I glanced back and forth at him. He was right, I did enjoy the sex, even if he did it to deceive me.

"Now that we work together, are you going to tell me your name?" I said.

He remained silent.

"It's not Marco like you told me, is it? I heard the Boss called you 'Griffin.' Is that your name?"

Still he said nothing.

"Fine, don't tell me. I'm calling you Biff then."

"Biff? Why Biff?"

"It suits you."

"Don't call me Biff."

"The first thing I need to do is learn how to hack. So I'm going to read some articles online, if that's all right with you, Biff."

His eyes shot daggers at me.

I read articles for a half-hour. Like almost everything on the Internet, it was full of generalities. I'd probably have to think my way through this.

Stretching out my arms, I yawned. "When's bedtime, Biff?"

In an instant he was out of his chair and grabbed my arm. "I said *don't* call me that."

I looked down at his hand. "If you hurt my arm, I'm not going to be able to use the computer."

He squeezed tighter. "You take a lot of chances, Jones." His grip loosened. "It's Griffin. My name is Griffin."

"Griffin?" Well, that did suit him, and far more than Biff ever did. "Is that your first or your last name?"

"Does it matter?"

I shrugged. "Suppose not."

Password cracking would be the key to getting this "Boss" the information he wanted, I decided. Tricking someone into compromising their password would be ideal, but I really had no idea how to go about doing that. As a coder, I probably could write up a program to determine the password; it could run from what appeared to the company's mainframe as multiple computers so that I wouldn't get locked out after trying thousands of wrong passwords while signing in.

When I looked at Griffin again, he crossed his legs and said, "Perhaps you would like to slip into something more comfortable?"

T-shirt and shorts did sound good right about then. The dress was extremely nice, but casual Saturday was more the programmer's uniform. It helped you get into the right frame of mind. "Sure."

He nodded toward the hallway. "The bedroom is at the end. I've taken the liberty of having clothes ordered for you."

My eyebrow rose. "Really?"

I went into the bedroom, where there awaited dozens of clothing boxes, all with names like Cosabella and Bluebella printed on them. The first box I opened contained a blue baby doll lingerie dress and the second a forest green deep V floral lace bodysuit. In fact, they all contained lingerie – teddies, strapless bustiers, chemises, camisoles, slip rompers – all made of fine satin, silk or lace. But not a damn blouse or pair of pants, never mind panties or bra, in the entire set.

What the fuck?

I went back to the computer center that I'm sure at one time was meant to be a living room.

Griffin looked up.

"So I'm supposed to be your private whore?" I said.

"I hope that we will be partners."

"Partners how? I hack into companies' computers wearing lingerie while you ogle me?"

"I'm your protector. While here, you'll want for nothing."

"Just my freedom."

He rose and in a single quick thrust of his arm, grabbed my throat. "You're too beautiful to be left to the creeps and low-lifes out there," he snarled. Fingers from his free hand gently ran along my collarbone then up my neck. "You deserve to be treated like a queen."

I murmured, and hoped to God that it wasn't out of pleasure.

Then his fingers slowly closed around my neck, as he leaned into my ear. "But that means I expect you to treat me like king," he said softly, as his fingers tightened into a noose. "If you don't, I'll throw you to those hyenas. *Comprende*?"

I nodded.

He slowly licked my ear as loosening his grip. "That's a good girl. Now you go back to the bedroom and pick out something to wear. Don't worry about the expenses; I've taken care of the bill."

"Yes sir," I squeaked out. He let go of my throat.

As I turned to leave, he swatted me on the butt. "You know," he said. "I think we're going to be a great team."

***

I decided to play along and donned the blue baby doll lingerie dress. And so there I sat at the computer, the unreachable summer lights of San Diego stretching beyond the window, Griffin's goofy grin and leering eyes in the easy chair, me writing a program that would relentlessly attempt to log into a company's computer systems until it succeeded. Committing a crime was better than the alternative, I supposed; after all, I'd seen some movie where kidnapped women were taken across the border and kept in the basement of some cartel mansion then made to "entertain" the boss's guests.

The program completed, I tested it on my computer at work. It didn't work, just kept trying to log in with the same password over and over. *Damn it.*

Griffin chuckled. "Having trouble?"

I glared at him. "Are you just going to sit there and stare at me?"

"I like watching you work."

"Well I don't. I can't concentrate when someone is staring at me."

"I'll get something to read."

You read?

He pulled out his cell phone and began tapping on it, then settled into scrolling down a screen. *Of course, you didn't mean read a book.*

After another half-hour of scanning through the program, I'd found the error. It worked on my next try, and that felt like a good place to stop or the night.

I looked up at Griffin, and though the memory of his hand wrapped around my throat still hovered in the front of my thoughts, I decided to be bold. "You didn't answer my question earlier."

"What question was that?"

"When is bedtime around here?"

"A party girl like you is tired already?"

"I was up late the last few nights."

He grinned. "I remember. First let me give you a tour of the place."

I followed him through the house. While the kitchen and

bathroom were well stocked, every other room was empty, except for two – the master bedroom and one bedroom containing tons of video gear.

"What is the filming equipment for?" I asked.

"The Boss used to run a porn film studio here."

My eyes widened. How many people had fucked in this house were now on Internet porn sites, DVDs, and streaming television channels? "He doesn't anymore though?"

Griffin laughed. "He got a better place and new equipment for it."

"Great, we get the leftovers."

He chuckled at that.

Once in the master bedroom, he began to undress. I took my chances and crawled under the covers still wearing the baby doll lingerie.

"So answer me this, kitten," he said. "How in the hell did you get in so much debt that you pissed off the Boss?"

"I needed the money for my aunt's surgery. She was going to die without it."

He laughed. "A do-gooder, huh? Is she still kickin' the can?"

"You're all heart. Yeah, she made it and is still going strong."

"And you got the loan with no intention of ever paying it back, right?"

"I didn't think they would find me."

He set his gun holster on the night stand. "The Boss finds everybody."

"How was I to know I was borrowing from some drug cartel? I went to a quick loan place in a strip mall."

He snorted. "All those quick loan places are run by drug cartels."

With that, he turned out the light and crawled into bed.

***

Despite being exhausted, I lay in the dark unable to sleep. That wasn't a problem for Griffin, though, as he spooned me, his arm wrapped around my waist and hand holding my breast while his hard cock pressed into my back. The pig. Hard to believe that less than 24 hours ago, before he drugged my drink, that I willingly sucked his cock and enjoyed it filling my pussy.

I assessed my situation. Apparently just Griffin was guarding me. If I had any hope of escape, I'd have to make sure he was out cold for a long time. I had no purse, no phone, no I.D., so I'd have to walk or hitchhike to some place safe, in lingerie no less. I pondered emailing for help, but no doubt they had someone monitoring my computer activity. Before the cops ever got here, there would be a bullet in my head.

My only hope rested in Alecia or my mother reporting me missing. Not that the police would ever find me here in this secluded mansion.

No, the only option was to quickly hack into the account like the Boss had asked so that I'd paid my debt. Then he'd let me go.

***

We sat across from one another at the breakfast table, plates of chipotle omelets and cups of black coffee before us. If I was going to escape before hacking into some company's computers, I'd have to come up with a way to get him to fall in love with me. Hopefully he was capable of love.

"Just what cartel do we work for, Griffin?" I took a bite of the omelet. Damn, my captor could cook.

65

"It's best that you don't know...for now anyway."

"You talked about us being partners."

He paused eating. "Would you like that?"

"Maybe. What does being *partners* mean?"

"It means we work as a team for the Boss. There are certain jobs he needs done that only a couple could do."

"A couple." He's thinking about being more than business partners. "So long as you do all of the cooking, our negotiations are off to a good start. This omelet is delicious."

He didn't react, just continued eating.

"How did you get involved in this cartel?" *If I can get him to open up about himself...*

"I had skills. When I proved to the Boss that those skills could be profitable to him, he took me into his organization."

Appropriately vague. But a start. "What were those skills?"

He gave a wide, V-shaped grin, and I shivered. "You just worry about the hacking."

We finished breakfast in silence. *Maybe I really don't want to know.*

***

I donned the purple chemise, as it covered a little more than the baby doll, but not by much. Then it was back to the computer. I set the program running on multiple "virtual" computers and went back to reading online articles on hacking in case I needed to take a different approach. Griffin scrolled through his phone until he went to make lunch.

Just before noon, one of the log-in attempts hit paydirt.

"I'm in," I said, maybe a little too gleefully.

Griffin looked in from the kitchen. "Really? That's excellent! Give me the log-in info."

66

I scribbled it on a piece of scratch paper and handed it to him.

Griffin tapped away on his phone. "Lunch is just about ready, take a seat."

A few minutes later, he brought two plates of *enchilades verdes* to the table.

I breathed in the succulent aroma. "You're going to make me fat."

He sat right next to me, started eating.

Then the enormity of what I'd done hit me. "I'm not sure I can eat."

"Why's that?"

"I'm confused. I'm proud of myself for actually doing this so quickly, yet I also feel guilty. I can't believe I just committed a major crime."

"Don't feel guilty," he said and brought his hand to my bare thigh. "Those companies steal from people like you and me every day."

"That doesn't make it right to–" but then I stopped, figuring he wouldn't see it my way. Besides, his fingers were dangerously close to my pussy, and I found my breathing starting to quicken. I needed to maintain control and recomposed myself. "What do we do now?"

"We wait."

"'Wait?' I did what he asked. You're not going to let me go?"

"The Boss needs to see if you actually got in their system."

"How long will that be?"

Griffin shrugged. "Might be all afternoon. Maybe tomorrow. When he gets to it."

"Look, I did what you asked. You can't keep me here."

"Would you prefer that I kill you? Because that's what the Boss will tell me do until he knows for certain that you've succeeded."

Rage pounded in my skull, wanting to break out. "I don't think you've thought this through. I can't keep missing work or someone eventually will come looking or report me missing."

He laughed. "The Boss not thinking something through? He thinks everything through."

"Well they will start looking for me when I miss that much work."

"You needn't worry about that. You resigned."

My face paled. "Resigned?"

"The Boss mailed your resignation letter a couple of days ago. They should have it by now."

"I can't quit my job – I need the money!"

He laughed. "The Boss is taking care of you now. He'll make sure you have all of the food and clothes you need."

"Clothes? You mean all the lingerie I need."

"Don't knock it. Those cute little numbers are the top of the line. And you do make them look good."

I suddenly felt hollow inside. "I'm never going to be released, am I?"

Griffin shook his head. "No."

***

I ran to the bedroom in tears. My life was over. I was their prisoner, and there was nothing I could do about it.

As I lay in the bed crying, Griffin came in and sat next to me. "I understand what you're going through," he said. "It was the same for me."

"What do you mean?" I choked out.

68

He reached for a box of tissue on the nightstand, handed it to me. "Like you, I didn't volunteer for this. I grew up in Nestor, didn't have a future. I was a bully and looking for any reason to start a fight. One night, I fought the wrong guy – one of the Boss's men. He went down fast, a couple of good left hooks and his head bounced off a concrete wall. Killed him."

Griffin placed his hand on my thigh again, began lightly trailing his fingers up it.

"The Boss's men hauled me in at gunpoint. He said if any other of his men had been killed, I'd be at the bottom of San Diego Bay. But the guy I beat up was his toughest man. Said he could use a strong man like me in his organization. So I had two choices – either swim the bay with my feet stuck in concrete or declare my loyalty to him and join his payroll."

His fingers lightly caressed the inside of my thighs, just below my pussy.

"So, like you, I didn't really have a choice."

I gazed into his garnet green eyes. *We're the same. That's why he wants to be my partner.*

Griffin pulled a tissue from the box and gently dabbed the tears from my cheeks as one of his fingers traced the folds of my pussy. "The Boss always rewards those who prove their worth. I don't lack for anything."

My breathing deepened, and his finger slipped inside me. I let go a low moan. Certainly he could tell I was wet from his teasing during lunch.

He rose from the bed, got on his knees at its side, and gripped my ankles. Pulling me to the mattress's edge, he pushed up the bottom of my chemise and his palms spread my thighs, fully exposing me to him.

His finger rubbed my labia and slit then dipped into my pussy. My neck arched, as I moaned again. He went deeper as I grew wetter then began thrusting his finger, as if it were his cock.

My hips ground against his finger as he thrust, then in went a second finger. I gasped, and he picked up speed, pistoning in and out of me.

Suddenly my muscles tensed, and my head arched back. "Oohh…" My whole body spasmed, as I came. I didn't think I ever could have a vaginal orgasm. *Damn him.*

As I came down from my high, he withdrew his fingers from me, and said, "See, we would be great partners."

***

I rolled away from him, closed my legs. "We'll never be partners."

His face paled, as if he'd just been kicked in the gut. "Don't, Serena. *Don't.*"

"Don't what?"

"Don't make me break you."

My heart stopped for a moment.

"Because I will. I'd rather have you come to me of your own accord, but if breaking you is what's required, I will."

"I'll never do anything more for this Boss. I'd rather be at the bottom of the bay."

Griffin rose, placed both hands on my hips and lifted me. I kicked, flailed my arms. "Let me go!"

He turned me over in the air, slammed me face down into the mattress. Before I could react, his big hand had both of my wrists and pulled my arms behind my back. The other yanked open the nightstand drawer and took something out. A moment later, I knew it was rope, as he wrapped it around my wrists and tied a knot. My legs kicked up, but the best I could do was smash the ball of my foot into his arm and back.

Once he'd secured my wrists, one of his hands went to the back of my neck, held me firmly in place. The other went to my pussy, where he pushed in a finger and swirled it around, as if dampening it with my juices. I tried kicking again, and he sat on one of my legs. Then his finger came out and slid upward to my ass.

He pressed the finger into me.

I gasped. It wasn't physically painful, other than a slightly uncomfortable pressure. But emotionally, I'd never felt anything more painful, as he violated my boundaries, my sense of worth.

"I'm doing this for your own safety," he said, as his finger pressed further into my ass. "You don't know what you're dealing with, but I do. I'm doing this because I don't want to see you hurt...because I don't want to see you dead.

"I'm doing this because I *love* you."

My gasps, muffled by the mattress, grew with each thrust of his finger inside me. I couldn't fight him off me, was at his mercy.

Griffin withdrew the finger from my ass, and I thought it was finally over. *He loves me,* I told myself, *and now he's going to fuck my pussy until we both cum. I can live with that...I want him inside right now.*

He reached for the nightstand drawer, and then came the click of plastic bottle cap popping off. Streams of lube splashed onto my ass, running down my crack and onto my pussy lips.

Griffin stood, and his belt unbuckled then his zipper came

down. Gripping my ankles, he bent my legs back toward me then with his hand swiped off some of the lube from my butt cheeks.

And then I felt his cock at my ass's entrance.

I gasped, and my eyes half rolled to the back of my head, as he pressed into me. I took a deep breath with every slow thrust he made, as he pushed deeper. My mouth bit the sheets to keep from screaming.

His speed picked up, and a ball of pleasure grew in my groin. His cock was so big that he was pressing my clitoris on the other side of my ass's canal, I realized. He had it about halfway in me – I wasn't sure that there was any more of me for him to fill – when my mouth let go of the sheets, and I moaned.

Then he pulled out, and I felt the air rush into my gaping ass. "I'm going to untie you," he said.

Griffin undid the rope holding my wrists, and I shook my hands to bring feeling back to them.

"Turn over," he said.

I rolled onto my back.

His big hands reached to the top of my chemise at my chest's center. He pulled the fabric and ripped, rending the two sides apart so that my breasts were exposed to him. It seemed like such a waste of expensive lingerie, yet the animalism of it left my heart racing.

Then his hands grabbed my ankles again and held my legs into the air, lifting my ass off the mattress. He stepped forward, so his cock stood at my ass's entrance, and slid in.

My eyes closed, as that ball of pleasure reappeared.

"Pull on your nipples," he said and began fucking my ass.

I pinched the skin around each nipple and pulled on them as

he thrust. The ball of pleasure grew larger, pulsing into my thighs and stomach. He grunted with each thrust, and in seconds my nipples were large and engorged as pleasure washed through my chest and lower legs. My neck arched farther back. If my eyes had been open, I would have been looking at the world upside down.

"I love you," he said, "and you love me." My whole body tensed.

With one last slam of his cock, he roared and spilled his warm cum deep into my ass. I spasmed, bucking against his buried cock. As floating in ecstasy, I thought, *I do love him.*

***

"Wake up. The Boss wants to see us. Wear the red dress you had on when you got here."

My ass ached, and I rubbed it as rising from the bed. "Is it good or bad?"

"Don't know. But if he was able to rob that company thanks to your work, I'd bet that it's good."

In the car, he blindfolded me again, and we went through the whole routine of Uzi guy and the butler packing heat. When he opened the twin oak doors, the Boss rose, smiling like he was some poor kid who just got his dream bicycle for Christmas.

"*Bienvenido!* Come in, come in." He went straight to the bar and poured three more glasses of that amber tequila then handed one to Griffin and one to me. "Miss Jones, I am impressed. Thanks to your work, you paid your debt at least three times over. Yes, we made quite a haul."

The Boss held up his glass in a toast, and we all clinked glasses.

Then he turned to Griffin. "And I'm impressed with you

seeing the value of Miss Jones to our organization. Joaquín never would have shown such vision." He turned back to me. "Did you know that Joaquín wanted to leave you dead in the desert? Well, he best be careful. I believe I've found my replacement for him should he fuck up."

Griffin merely nodded once in acknowledgement.

"Well, Miss Jones, I suspect you think you're free to go now, don't you?"

"Actually..." I tried to remember the exact words Griffin told me I should say. "I'd like to see if you have more work for me to do."

The Boss grinned then patted my cheek. "I see that you're a very intelligent woman, Miss Jones. Either that, or Griffin talked some sense into you." He winked at Griffin. "As a matter of fact, I do, Miss Jones. When you return to the hacienda, you'll find the instructions for that job on your keyboard."

"Thank you, sir."

"Ah, so formal! Call me 'Boss.' You're one of us now!" He took a long, leering look at me. "Perhaps one day you'll even work here, close to me." He chuckled then gulped down his tequila.

Griffin and I followed in kind.

"Take the evening off, go have some fun," the Boss said. "You can start the new operation in the morning. Hopefully, I will see you in another week for more good news."

With that, the Boss went back to his desk and began reading through a stack of papers on it. The packing butler hurried us into the hallway.

At the car, Griffin tied the blindfold around me eyes. The door clicked open, and placing his hand on my head and another on my ass, he guided me in, then came the *whump* of the door closing. I suddenly felt claustrophobic.

Getting into the car, Griffin turned the ignition. "That went well, kitten. You did good, and the Boss likes you. Hopefully that is incentive enough for you to continue our partnership."

My stomach churned. "Griffin, tell me..." I couldn't ask him.

"Tell you what, kitten?"

I didn't say anything though I needed to hear it, just to keep going on.

His large hand gently cupped my cheek. "Oh kitten, it's all right. I love you, remember?"

I nodded. "And I love you," I said, almost robotically.

He patted my cheek. "That's a good girl. We're going to be great partners."

With that, he put the car into gear, and we drove off into uncertainty.

Red is the Rose

The moment I placed my hand on the door handle, I stood along the border of possibility. On the other side, somewhere in the Irish pub, sat Nathanael, waiting to see what I'd do. My daughter's father-in-law had presented it as an invite, but I read it as a dare.

I took the challenge.

Heat and the rowdy laughter of drinkers washed over me as the door opened. What little light there was in Houligans glinted off the sparkling green St. Patrick's Day decorations and a couple of the patrons' leprechaun hats. I scanned the bar for Nathanael then spotted him waving at me from a booth tucked in a corner.

He smiled as I approached then gestured to take a seat across from him. Though understated, his crow's feet wrinkled pleasantly. His thick dirty blond hair further de-aged him.

"You sure make that green dress look good, Desirae."

I grinned. He always knew the right words to say, just like his son. "I see you didn't dress for the holiday."

"Green really isn't my color."

"That's not what your emerald eyes suggest."

His smile grew then he waved for the waitress. I ordered a Guiness in a glass.

Once the waitress left, I said, "What would your son say if he knew you were on a date with his wife's mother?"

"Probably what your daughter would say if she knew you were on a date with her husband's father."

My grin widened. That Nathanael and I were interested in one another only made sense by my way of thinking. Children often found attractive the same qualities in the opposite sex that their parents did. A son wants a girl just like the girl that married dear old dad; a daughter wants a boy like the boy that married dear old mom. So Nathanael must like women who are similar to the woman his son fell in love with...and who could be more similar to said woman than her mother? That Nathanael and I had both divorced our children's other parent made little difference in the equation.

The waitress returned with my beer. Nathanael quickly told her to put it on his tab, and then she was off.

"Are you trying to get me drunk?" I said.

His face pinkened. "I'll be sure to cut you off at a dozen."

I sipped my beer – a smooth, creamy sweetness balanced with a hoppy bitterness – as we talked aimlessly about what was going on where we worked, upcoming vacation plans, and the latest thoughts are reorganizing our homes now that we were empty nesters. Listening to his deep, resonant voice, I imagined him nuzzling the nape of my neck with his warm mouth, of whispering sweet nothings in my ear, of his fingertips grazing along the side of my waist, of his hand cupping my ass and pressing me against his hardness. A heat surged in my chest, and I drank the last swallow of beer in my glass to steady myself. He signaled the waitress for a refill. I slipped off my pumps and slowly ran the sole of my foot over his calf.

Nathanael leaned toward me, and despite that I'd worn a

dress flaunting my cleavage, he kept his eyes locked on mine as we conversed. *Good boy.* My foot creeped to his knee, massaged it. His breathing grew shallow, though he tried not to show he was turned on. The waitress returned with my refill, but I kept my sole on his leg.

She no sooner left than a heavy-set man dressed in traditional a grandfather shirt, ankle-length trousers, and flat wool cap, stepped up to the table. "Nathanael! You're not playing tonight?"

"Kieran! Are you the entertainment this evening?"

"Entertainment may be too strong of a word for it." He laughed. "And who is this lovely lady?"

"Kieran, this is Desirae. Desirae – Kieran."

"That's not an Irish name," he said to me, "but I'm glad to see you're in the spirit wearing green." He turned back to Nathanael. "You should play a number with us tonight."

"Oh, I don't know–"

"You play Irish instruments?" I asked.

Nathanael shook his head. "Guitar."

"And he plays it better than the rest of us play our traditional instruments," Kieran piped up. "He would be doing us a favor."

"Well, if it's all right with Desirae," Nathanael said. "I wouldn't want to leave her alone."

"I don't blame you," Kieran said to him. "Just one number so none of these muppets here have a chance to spirit off your lovely lady."

"I'd love to hear you play," I said.

"Then count me in."

"We're about to start; come up with me," Kieran said then

turned my way. "And you too – I'll find you a nice spot to sit so you can make sure he isn't foolin' around with any of the cailíní." He winked.

We squeezed our way through the crowd to the makeshift stage at the pub's side.

"Broderick – fetch the guitar from the basement," Kieran said. "Nathaniel is playing a number with us."

Then he walked up to a man sitting on a barstool in sight of the stage.

"Sir, this fine young lady would like to hear just one number from our troupe. If you would be willing to give up your seat to her for that number, I'd be happy to buy you a beer and give you the privilege of standing next to her during that song."

"Sha!" the man said and rose from the stool.

"Thank you sir," Kieran said and signaled the bartender to serve him a beer.

Broderick returned with the guitar, which Nathaniel strummed a little then adjusted one of the knobs on the headstock.

"Welcome – we're the Blarney Boys," Kieran said into the microphone. "Tonight we have a special guest performer, all the way from Kerry Patch – Nathaniel Brennan sitting in with us for a number."

The band whispered among themselves for a moment, then Nathanael, gazing at the guitar strings, began playing, a soft pastoral melody and within a couple of notes the flutist joined him. I stared at his handsome, square jaw as the stage lights shined on him, then he began singing:

Come over the hills my bonnie Irish lass

Come over the hills to your darling
You choose the road love, and I'll make the vow
And I'll be your true love forever

He looked up at me, stared with his emerald green eyes, as the other singers joined in the chorus:

Red is the rose that in yonder garden grows
Fair is the lily of the valley
Clear is the water that flows from the Boyne
But my love is fairer than any

A longful heat crept across my chest. He caught my gaze and held it as singing. Then he looked at Kieran playing the fiddle. I watched Nathanael's fingers move delicately over the strings, as if he were touching something precious, something sacred, each shift and flick producing a powerful note that reverberated across the room. I imagined his fingers upon my body, artfully bringing me to ecstasy.

Twas down by Killarney's green woods that we strayed
When the moon and the stars they were shining
The moon shone its rays on her locks of golden hair
And she swore she'd be my love forever

I thought of how my daughter told me of when she'd first seen Nathanael's son play guitar. She couldn't stop gushing about it, was even turned on a little by it I thought at the time, and as Nathanael played before me, I understood why. A warmth in my breasts traveled to my tummy then to between my legs and along my derrière.

The band broke into the chorus, then sang the final verse:

Tis not for the parting with my sister Kate
Tis not for the grief of my mother
Tis all for the loss of my bonnie Irish lass
That my heart is breaking forever

Then came the chorus and a repeat of it, the last one more rousing. When the band finished, applause and cheers rose from the crowd.

"Yes! Nathanael Brennan everyone!" Kieran shouted in the mic as waving a hand toward him.

Nathanael stood and bowed, and another round of applause came. He held up the guitar, said something to Kieran then stepped off the stage. The band began a new number as Nathanael approached me.

"That was beautiful!" I said as standing.

He kissed my cheek as touching my arm. "Thank you. I promised to bring the guitar back to the basement. Come with me?"

I nodded, and we were off to a door tucked next to the restrooms. When Nathanael opened it, a black hole appeared before us, and he flicked on a light that barely brightened the darkness. Another possibility awaited. He closed the door behind me, and we descended the stairs.

"I knew you played guitar, but I didn't know you were so good," I said. "Like father like son, I guess."

He chuckled as placing the guitar into a case and snapping it shut. A keyboard, tambourine, and a couple of speakers stood next to the concrete block wall.

Rising, he said, "Can I say like mother like daughter as well?"

"You can. For most things anyway."

He gazed at my face a long moment. "My son tells me a lot about his relationship with his wife. I guess we've always had a close relationship like that."

"My daughter and I are the same way. And when not, often she infers what's on her mind simply by asking questions. A mother knows."

Nathanael came close to me, so we were only an inch apart, as we stared into one another's eyes. His hand tilted my chin up, then he captured my lips with his own. The kiss was slow at first, tender and reverent, as though he were memorizing the taste of me.

As our bodies pressed against another, the softness of my lips beneath his, we wrapped our arms around one another. His cock grew beneath his dress pants, and I grinded in a slow circle against him, encouraging it.

Nathanael let out a soft sigh, and I rubbed up and down his erection until through our clothes it slid between the lips of my cleft. He moaned, and my heart beating faster. I sped up. His large hand slid down my waist to my ass, cupped a cheek and pressed me against his erection.

I slowed down my grinding then suddenly sped up again, and he gasped. His free hand went to my other ass cheek, and as his breathing deepened, he ground against me. Closing my eyes, I bit my lower lip, his excitement leaving my chest and face flushed with heat.

In a lone, swift motion, one of his arms lowered itself to the behind my knees as the other pressed against my back, and he raised me up. I squealed in delight, then he backed me to the basement wall, and lowering me went to his knees.

"Lift your dress," he ordered.

I tugged it up to my waist, as he pulled down my panties. Nathanael kissed my cleft then sucked each lip into my mouth, savoring them – no, worshipping them. I thrust my hip up so my ass was not fully pressed against the wall, as his tongue swiped up and down my pussy, separating it. A moment later, his tongue found my clit, flicked it in a way that almost any woman's back would arch as she moaned. Yes, his warm, wet mouth did feel good down there, but it wasn't what I wanted.

Still, I let him do as he pleased; I didn't want to disappoint him, so faked a gasp. He slid a finger into the opening of my pussy, swirled around it then pushed a little farther. My vaginal juices flowed, and as his tongue flicked against my clit, he kept pushing his finger further, until it was all the way in. I squeezed it with my muscles, teased it a moment by keeping it there.

When I let go, his finger withdrew then reached behind my pussy, slid up my ass's divide, and ran slow, gentle circles around my netherhole. My eyes rolled to the back of my head, as I moaned. He pressed against the opening, slid in to the end of his nail.

Soon he has it in half-way then all the way and thrusting it in and out. My sphincter relaxed, allowing him easy access, as his finger pressed my clitoris hidden through the anal cavity's walls. My mouth widened, as I whimpered in pleasure. Eyes closed, I brought my pinkie to my own mouth, sucking on its tip.

I pushed down on his finger, gasping the deeper it went. Then my body froze up, as I moaned and went limp. The orgasm was light, like a quick spray of water during a hot day. I sighed, and his tongue and his finger left me.

Dizzy, I let him guide me to a board held up by two barrels, which he bent me over. He unbuckled his belt and pants, and once they hit the floor, he tossed my dress over my waist then spread my ass checks.

"What a beautiful flower you have, Desirae. So red is the rose."

His spongy cockhead pressed against my netherhole.

How did he know that's what I wanted? Of course he'd know. *"My son tells me a lot about his relationship with his wife," he'd said.*

I winced at the initial pressure, a necessary discomfort on the way to pleasure, like that moment your stomach falls as the carnival ride begins its ascent. Nathanael kept pushing forward, gently though, letting my ass get used to his size. Slowly the joy of it – feeling so filled, his cock pressing and rubbing against more of my internal clitoris than his finger ever could – overtook me. As he gripped my waist, the sphincter muscle relaxed, and then he was a third of the way in.

I gasped then found myself floating higher and higher. He was halfway in and gradually fucking me faster and faster and faster until I was as high as the mountains and could barely catch my breath. My nails dug into the board, then he was all the way in me and hitting my A-spot.

My head arched back as I moaned, my muscles tightened, as if the coils of a spring pressed in on itself, then they tightened even more, and suddenly ecstasy rippled deeply through me. The tension released from all of my muscles all at once, as my whole body spasmed, and I screamed, "Oh yes! Yes!"

That threw him over the edge, as he made one last thrust then, growling while his large hands tightened on my waist, and his warm cum spurt into me.

We remained locked together, both quiet, until catching our breaths. At last, he backed off me, and I turned around, pulling up my panties and straightening my dress.

"Looks like we share a common interest with our children," I said.

"I wasn't sure," he said. "Especially when you said you and your daughter were alike in *most* ways. 'But maybe not that one way,' I thought."

"I'm glad you continued the chase. Such a fetish is not something usually discussed on a first date. Often a talk never occurs at all."

He'd pulled up his pants by then. "I'm rather open about such matters. I enjoy the front side as well, but the back, being much smaller, is an exquisite feeling."

"I've discovered down the years that for me anal sex occupies the space in my life that vaginal sex does for others. From my earliest teenage memories, I was really only turned on by the thought of anal play."

"I understand," he said, and we kissed, soft and languidly. "Well, shall we head back up?"

I nodded then my finger playfully circled his chest. "But let's not stay here. We still have much to discover about one another."

He grinned then took my hand, and we ascended the stairs to the closed door, beyond which yet more possibilities awaited.

Supergirl

I tried not to stare at him. His beefy arms pushed up what must have been 200 pounds on the bench press, and he grunted on the last rep then left it racked. Sitting up to rest, his tall muscular physique was as perfect as a Michelangelo original. I tried to avoid staring at him by concentrating on my own workout, but that was impossible once he started lifting again. As he hefted the weights, his dark hair shined in the early morning sunlight breaking through the fitness club's windows. *I'm above this,* I told myself, *I wouldn't fall for a man just because he looks like a model from some trashy romance cover.*

That no one was spotting him surprised me, but he didn't appear to have any trouble raising the weight. Maybe he was the loner type. I tried focusing on my incline presses, limiting myself to only an occasional out-of-the-corner-of-my-eye glance his way.

Eventually, I forced myself to leave that part of gym and settled for the cable machine across from a floor-to-ceiling mirror. As doing lat pulldowns, I stared at myself in the mirror, not focusing at all on my exercise's form but the spandex capris and a jog bra with my long, straight hair falling to it. There weren't any curves at all to hide or accentuate. No wonder I was still single. I was just another skinny gal trying to get a Supergirl figure.

Then I remembered my friend Kiarra once mentioned that she'd met a man named Matthew in the gym. He had an impressive build, dark hair, and was nice guy, easy to talk to. I wondered if this was the same guy and went back to the bench press across from where he was lifting more than 200 pounds.

When he racked the weight and sat up, I was watching him, and his eyes met mine. He smiled and said "Hi."

Tongue-tied, I barely managed to squeak out a "Hi" in return.

"Emma, right?"

Wait, how did he know who I was?

"I'm Matthew." His eyes roved over me as he spoke. He stood, and for a moment I thought I was in the presence of a giant. His gray Providence Marina T-shirt hugged a muscle on every part of his broad shouldered torso, atop which was a chiseled face with ocean blue eyes you wanted to drown in.

Of course, she'd also told him about me. *C'mon, think fast on your feet.* "I thought you might be that guy Kiarra mentioned. I couldn't remember your name." *Liar.*

"She said all good things I hope."

"Maybe I'd prefer to hear the bad things." *I can't believe I said that.*

He grinned like a naughty boy who'd just been caught. "Well, Kiarra only said good things about you."

"Well, darn it." *Quit flirting!*

Matthew chuckled. "I don't think I've seen you here before."

"I'm an *ir*regular."

He smiled. "If you're looking for a personal trainer, I'd be happy to help. For free of course."

Hmm, he might have just given me a good reason to start

coming here more often. "I'm interested."

"Awesome. Do you have a workout routine?"

I blushed. "No, I just sort of follow what I see everyone else doing."

"Sometimes that works, and you're certainly in good shape. But if you have a specific goal in mind for your body, then you can tailor your workouts to it and get the kind of body you want more quickly. So what kind of body are you aiming for?"

Half of my brain said, *Stop mansplaining,* but the louder portion said, *What kind of body do you want me to have?*

"I guess I'm the skinny girl trying to build curves."

He nodded. "Start by sculpting your shoulders. It'll make your hips appear smaller and cause your..." He paused a moment. "...*bosom* to thrust out more."

"That sounds good."

"Here, try these dumbbells." He went to the weight rack and brought me two 5-pounders."

Matthew had me stand tall with arms hanging by my sides and a dumbbell in each hand. Then he told me to perform a bicep curl by bringing the weights up to my shoulders, which he mimicked with his own massive arms. Christ, each one looked like it was the size of my thigh.

His hands gently took hold of my wrists and brought me through the motion. As his fingers ran up the length of my forearm, he left a wake of goosebumps behind them, then he reached my elbow. I breathed in his scent, a mix of cinnamon and smooth bourbon.

"Good. Don't lock the elbows. Now bring the dumbbells down to your shoulders, rotate the palms so they face you..." His hands guided me through this motion as well, leaving my body electrified. "Next slowly bring the arms back down to their start position. Do nine more of those."

My Adonis stepped back, watched me. When my arms were over my head, my small breasts fully jutted out, and I wondered for a moment if this was some pervy trick he was playing on me. Then I felt the burn in my shoulders.

When done, I set the dumbbells back on the rack. "That really got my shoulder muscles feeling something," I said. *Not to mention other body parts.*

"Your form looked good," he said. *Double entendre?* "Hey, I have to clean up and go to work. Let's get together again, Wednesday at 6. I'll put together a workout plan for you, cool?"

I nodded. "Cool. See you then."

I watched him walk off, admired his perky butt.

Then I pondered if he really was Kiarra's Matthew. He easily could
have overhead my name when I checked in that morning and just played along. Not once did he say her name.

There was only one way to find out.

I quick snuck to a machine he'd passed, and just before he went into the men's locker room, snapped a pic of him.

***

"So does that look like him?" I said to Kiarra on my phone.

"Sure does, though without seeing the face, it could be someone who is *like* him. Hmm...if it is him, he packed on even more muscle. I didn't think that was possible."

"So you think he is...interested in me?" *Because I'm sure interested in him, though I shouldn't be.*

"If any other guy took the time to help you with a workout plan, I'd say yes. But with Matthew... well, he's a nice guy, and that's just the kind of thing he would do, even if he *isn't* interested in you."

"That doesn't sound very promising."

Kiarra sighed. "I would have been happy to sleep with him. But I kept getting mixed signals. We never even met for coffee."

"Do you think he's...gay?"

"Maybe. I dunno. I've never seen him make moves on a guy or even look at one."

"Would be a loss for the sisterhood if he was."

***

Wednesday morning couldn't come quickly enough, and I hated myself for feeling that way. It's not that I'd never been excited about a guy before, just that I was more thrilled about his perfect body than him as a human being. Educated, adult women shouldn't think that way, right?

As I stretched out near the mirrors, Matthew marched in wearing gym clothes that accentuated his wide chest, bulging arms, and thick legs.

"Hey," he said then nodded as a way of a greeting. "If you want to give me your number, I'll text over the workout plan I have for you."

He handed me his phone. I hesitated, pondering what this might mean, then typed it in. A few seconds later, a text from him arrived. There was nothing in it, not even an emoji, just an attachment with a day-by-day list of exercises.

"What's 'IT?'"

"Interval Training," he said.

"Sounds intense."

"It could be. Shall we start?"

"Aren't you going to do your workout?"

"It's my week off. It's important to rest the muscles and let them heal."

Great – I get his full attention for the week ahead! "Okay, what's first?"

"Squats."

"I never do 'em."

"We'll start without weights, just get the form down."

We walked over to the floor to ceiling mirror. He demonstrated then had me imitate.

"Let the hip and knee joints flex when you go down," he said. "Good. Keep the back straight."

He placed a hand on my mid back and another on my stomach. "Okay, go down again."

As I did, his hands kept me from leaning my back forward. I slightly bent at the knees to stay level with me. I thought about going lower than he'd showed me so that his hand would brush the bottom of my breasts.

Stop it! I told myself.

As continuing the squats, I asked, "Where do you work?"

"Ridge Software. Director of Marketing. You?"

"Grayer Corp. Sales Manager."

"Impressive."

"Not as much as it sounds," I chuckled and finished the squats.

"It's fairly dull."

"Just thank the stars that you're not a plumber. It's a crappy job."

I laughed. *Wait, is he actually flirting?*

"Next up is walking lunges," he said. *Hmm, all business again, probably not flirting.*

He took me through the motions, this time just doing the lunges along with me. Given that Kiarra had said he wasn't married, I needed to choose my next words carefully. As we moved forward, I said, "With all of the working out you do each morning, your girlfriend must appreciate not having to make you breakfast."

"Oh, there's no girlfriend," he said. "All right, looks like you're workout is smooth sailing so far; let's go over to the leg press."

Still all business. If asking about a girlfriend isn't hint enough, then I didn't know what will be.

I reclined on the bench and placed my feet on the push plate, as he racked the leg press machine.

"All right, push," he said. "Okay, don't lock the knees. Keep them flexed." He placed a hand underneath my calf just below the knee and the other atop the thigh just above the knee. "Okay, push."

Before my leg was about the fully stretch, his hands firmed on my leg.

"That's where you want to stop pushing," he said. "If you lock your knees, you could pull a muscle, or the knee itself could buckle."

After a couple of more reps of doing it right, his hands left my legs. For a moment, I thought about deliberately locking my knees just so he'd touch me again. But I resisted and focused on the exercise.

"That looks great," he said, as I pressed. "You look like Supergirl!"

***

I sat in my office, feeling fire in my legs, as thoughts of

Matthew burned in my head. Men with perfect bodies don't keep me up nights, don't make my body tingle, don't dampen my private parts, don't compel me to make moronic decisions driven by passion, I told myself. No, that's not at all what was supposed to be sexy about men.

Carrie, the department's assistant manager, ducked her head into my office. "Trace and Jakob are arguing over a lead. Trace said he's already worked on them last year, and they won't bite, but Jakob when he made a cold call to them yesterday said they were interested. The company matches our profile customer, and I think Trace is just worried he won't get credit if Jakob lands them–"

I held up my hand, for Carrie had a way of talking forever. Besides, I already knew the answer. "Tell Jakob if he lands them as a client, he gets the commission, but that I don't want him spending too much time on them. Trace is a damn good sales rep, and if he couldn't land them last year, they're probably just playing us so they can get a better deal from their current supplier. If they don't sign on by the end of next week, Jakob should let them go."

"That makes perfect sense – no wonder you're the boss!" and she was off.

Back to sales reports, I told myself. A few lines in, my mind drifted to Matthew's fingers grazing the length of my leg, as I did extensions that morning. Then snapping back to the report, I half-growled. *Apparently I'm not the boss of my thoughts.*

I focused again on the reports. Looks like Andy was down last month. That new account he landed should make up for it a few months, though. I'll have to keep an eye on that.

Then I thought about Matthew raising his bar with 200

pounds of weights on it, of his huge arm muscles flexing, as sweat glistened on them.

What on Earth am I doing? He's not interested in me. If he was, he'd already have asked me out for coffee or dinner. Focus, Emma, focus!

My attention went back to the sales report. Numbers were up for June, except for Andy's, but everyone else more than made up for it. Though the Fourth of July was on a Saturday, the holiday still would dampen this month's first week figures, so I wouldn't know if we were on track to equal June's numbers until the week of the 10th.

That's the week Matthew starts working out again.

I cursed myself for the distraction, decided to read a more interesting report to help me stay focused. I clicked tabs for various spreadsheets, trying to find one. *Ah, the sales call report.*

Liz had a good ratio of created leads to outbound calls, while Andy's total number of calls was down, no doubt due to his focus on landing Metpipe as a client. Inbound calls overall were up, and I felt Matthew's hand underneath my calf. He smiled boyishly, as if about to do something naughty, as his eyes studied me with desire. Naked, I pushed the leg press plate, and my stretched, parted legs revealing the dampness between my–

Goddamnit! I hissed between my teeth.

Grabbing my smartphone, I scurried to the women's restroom. *Good, no one is here.* I took the empty stall at the far end, hiked down both skirt and panties, and sat on the toilet. My finger found the photo of him on my phone, and I stared at his giant muscles on that sculpted body, as another finger found my slit.

Sliding up and down it, gradually I pressed deeper until my finger was as slick as my folds. I set down the phone. Eyes closed, a second later the finger reached my clit and, slowly flicked it. Matthew's hand caressed a breast, as I let out a soft moan, while his other hand concentrated on my clit, brushing it in a gentle strokes. My breathing quickened.

Then his finger entered my vagina, thrusted slowly in and out of it. My head arched back as a leg rose and its foot rested on the toilet paper dispenser. His other finger pressed on my clit, circled it, as a second finger slipped into me.

His thrusting and circling accelerated, and every muscle in my body tensed. I let out an incredible gasp, and for a moment my body floated.

At last, I come down to earth, and my breathing softened.

A superorgasm for Supergirl.

***

We worked out again Friday morning, and at the end of it, I found
myself wondering how I'd be able to stand not seeing Matthew until Wednesday with the three-day weekend ahead. There still was no invite to go out; despite having my number, he hadn't phoned or texted once. *That should tell you something*, I told myself. *He's probably playing me just like that company is playing Jakob.*

During that morning's workout, Matthew mentioned living in the Fox Point neighborhood down by the marina, and as I alternated between sales reports and thoughts of him caressing me with his large hands, a thought struck me. Fox Point was where Brew HaHa Coffeeshop was. Everybody heading out on the water stopped there for morning coffee.

So why not me as well?

My internal voice said, *C'mon, Emma, that's stalking him.*

I may not even see him, I responded. I'm not exactly following him around.

If he wants to go out with you, he'll ask.

Men are dumb, I told myself. Sometimes they need a nudge.

He's all wrong for you. You just like him because he's incredibly hot.

We would just have coffee together. Is that wrong?

Go ahead. You'll see I'm right.

The Brew HaHa bustled with activity when I walked in that warm sunny morning, dressed in a cheery sundress and sandals. Partially blinded by the coffeeshop's dimness and not really familiar with the layout – I'd only been there once or twice – I stood at the entry for a moment. Well, maybe for several moments, trying not to lose my nerve.

C'mon Emma, quit acting like you've got a finger stuck up your butt.

I spotted him, though his head was buried in his phone. So I ordered a latte, every once in a while glanced his way, and when my order was up, took it to a spot where he could see me if he looked up, and just stood there, acting like I was searching for a place to sit.

At last he did look. His eyes lit up. "Hi Emma, care to join me?"

"Oh Matthew, what a nice surprise," I said and took a seat.

"I didn't know you lived in the area."

"I don't. Just wanted to take a walk along the river. It's a beautiful day."

"Yes, the perfect Fourth. Clear skies tonight for the fireworks."

We could have fireworks no matter what the weather.

We talked for the longest time about anything and nothing really – our jobs, in which a comment about business conferences in other cities led to where we'd traveled, which somehow morphed into my hobby of reading mysteries and his like of Patrick O'Brian's novels, which led to his interest in boating. No, his *passion* for boating actually.

He leaned back in his chair, his muscles rippling under his baby blue T-shirt that brought out the color in his eyes. "Say, are you doing anything today?"

"No, not all."

"Want to check out my boat?"

Fuck yeah! "That sounds nice."

He rose. "It's a short walk from here."

Guess he's not playing me at all.

***

Except maybe he was. As we walked Bridge Street to the marina, he didn't try to hold my hand. Or compliment my outfit. Or anything at all.

We walked out on the wooden dock with boats on either side, the boards clacking beneath us as the turquoise lake spread out wide and a seagull dipped rose into the sky. At the dock's end, Matthew stopped and waved his hand at a boat. "Here she is."

Gleaming white in the sun, it must have ran 40 feet long or so and looked like it had an interior. When he said he was into boating, I thought he meant like a small motorboat. This damn thing was almost a yacht and had so many ropes on it I couldn't make out where they all came from and ran to.

Hmm, ropes.

"I'd be happy to give you a ride," he said.

Not quite the ride I had in mind. Despite half-stalking him at the coffeeshop and our enjoyable conversation, I debated if I should take him up on his offer. *If I go, I may throw myself at him. Of course, if I don't go, I'm telling him I'm not interested.*

Well, you aren't interested in him. You're just enamored with his body.

Oh, and what a body it is.

"Yeah, that'd be fun," I said at last.

He smiled boyishly and stepped onto the behemoth then offered me a hand. My fingers were tiny in his palm, and I got on deck beside him. The boat didn't wobble as much as I thought it might.

He started showing me around, pointing out where he piloted it from and then took me to a set of three steep steps heading into the interior. I ducked my head and stepped inside. There was a small kitchen, a table with a cushioned booth around half of it, and a bed, all surrounded by warm-colored wood.

"You could live in this!" I exclaimed.

He chuckled. "I've often thought about it."

The boat must have cost him a pretty penny. With all of his time spent working out, boating, and working to pay for his hobby, no wonder he didn't have a girlfriend. I quick glanced around for any women's paraphernalia, just to make sure I wasn't one in a long string of conquests.

"I'll take you out on the water, and we'll have lunch," he said.

I nodded, and he untied the ropes mooring his boat to the

dock. The ropes looked taut, yet his muscular hands and arms had no trouble loosening them. After a few moments, we were free upon the water, and he started the engine.

We putted into the Providence River's main current then headed toward the ocean, passing houses and small public beaches along the way. After a few minutes, we reached an island where the shoreline around a secluded cove was wooded, and he killed the engine and tossed a small anchor. All that broke the quiet was the casual wash of waves against the boat, the occasional rustle of tree leaves, and a bird whistling some love tune.

He set up a couple of chairs at the front of the boat then went into a cabin, a moment later bringing up some pre-made sandwiches and cut fruit accompanied by a couple of beers.

"Hope you like ham," he said as handing me sandwich. "I was planning to spend the day out here alone but am glad you came along."

"What do you out here by yourself?"

"Eat lunch." He bit into his sandwich and when done chewing continued. "Fish sometimes. Sleep a bit under the sun. Just enjoy the silence."

It sounded boring as hell. I was a shopper, a foodie. I liked to accumulate clothes, experiences, sales leads. *Matthew and I aren't meant for one another.*

But we ate and talked. He showed me how to fish, which actually was more fun than I thought it would be. We had another beer. I admired his muscular build.

"You're starting to get sunburned," I said.

"You too. Sorry, I got distracted and forgot all about sunscreen. I've got some in the cabin." He ambled down into it.

Distracted? By what? We're just floating.

Once back on the deck, he applied the sunscreen to his face and arms then handed me a tube. "Would you mind putting some on my back? I can't quite reach there."

"Sure."

He reached behind his neck and grabbing his collar pulled the T-shirt straight over his head, revealing a set of chiseled abs and his chest, which looked like hard granite.

Then he sat on the deck, and I got on my knees behind him. I squirted a small amount of the creamy sunscreen on my hands then rubbed them together so it was spread evenly. My hands moved slowly across his shoulders, and after a couple of seconds he relaxed. I moved up to his neck and then the upper back, felt his thick muscles in my fingers and palms. The sunscreen didn't seem to have a scent of its own, allowing me to breathe in his, that wonderful intoxicating cinnamon and smooth bourbon. My hands made circular motions across his skin as rubbing downward to his lower back, just above his shorts. I patted his shoulders, then my fingers trailed down the side of his abs.

"That felt good," he said. "Thanks."

Nodding, I screwed back on the sunscreen cap. As much as I wanted to further explore his gorgeous body, he remained polite and kept his distance. He never made a move on me and didn't flirt. I was disappointed because I'd hoped this would be the beginning of something memorable. Why had he invited me to his boat? What were his intentions?

I needed to press the issue.

He sat there, as I came around to his front. "Perhaps you could return the favor," I said.

"Of course." I held out the sunscreen for him to take, and as he reached, I caught a glimpse of the bulge in his shorts.

Okay, he's not gay.

"All right then," I said, kicking off my sandals. "My turn."

***

I reached behind my back and slowly unbuttoned my sundress then in a single motion shrugged so it fell to the boat deck.

His eyes slowly widened, but he said nothing. I unclasped my bra, let it tumble off so I stood there only in my black satin panties. "Do you have a blanket for me to lay on?"

He went to the cabin and brought up a lightly colored plaid one with a small pillow to rest my head on. I got comfortable atop it, the sun warm upon my back, the waves gently lapping against the shore, and occasional bird tweet like soft, soothing music.

Matthew placed a hand on my shoulder and kneaded his thumbs deep into its muscles. Then he worked his way up along the neck, all the way to the hairline. He moved around to my front and with his hands in a fist, gently but firmly rubbed the knuckles across my shoulder tops, releasing all the tension in them.

Then he moved back to my feet, wrapped both hands around them and with his thumbs massaged their soles. He paid special attention to the arch of each foot, then when he got to the toes, gripped each one individually, pulling gently.

"Matthew, can I ask you something? Why didn't you text me? Or ask me out?"

"You didn't seem interested."

"Oh…" Maybe I was too cautious. "I *was. Am.*"

102

He worked his way up my legs, giving each long, relaxing strokes then he kneaded both calves like they were bread dough. Pressing the heel of his hand, he very slowly moved up the thighs.

"I don't mean to sound arrogant, but a lot of women are interested, mainly for my body," he said. "They just want to jump in the sack though."

"You'd think a man would be happy about that," I responded, as his hand moved to my lower back and worked their way up each side of the spine.

"That's like launching a marketing campaign in which people only want your free samples but never buy."

Apt. "And what does buying look like?" Sales is my department after all.

"I want someone I can confide in. Someone to protect."

"You truly are a unique man, Matthew."

His hands fanned outwards across my shoulders, and he kneaded down to the lower back. He pressed his fingertips into the flesh then quickly released. Tension left my body, as if I were in a warm, luxurious bath.

I told myself that this isn't just banging some guy you find physically attractive but that he's nice, that he's easy to talk to, that he makes me laugh. Those are the right ingredients aren't they?

"And what if I said I was willing to be your confidante?" I said. "Would that get me a... *sample* of the merchandise?"

***

His thumbs hooked into the sides of my panties' waistband and pulled them down my legs. *I guess the answer is yes.*

Then his large hands placed themselves on my inner legs

and parted them, exposing my pussy to him. His fingers glided over my folds then his thumb ran along my slit, and I moaned.

"You're already wet," he said.

"Hmm-mm."

His thumb slid in and an instant later found my clit. With his large hands, he could hardly miss it. An electric tingle ran through my body, growing in intensity, as he slowly circled my love nub. My breathing deepened, and I murmured in pleasure. He swiped the inside of my folds with his palm then went back to circling the clit.

Then his thumb teased the rim of my vagina, massaged it, and pushed in, and I let out a long moan. Pulling it out, bringing my juices with it, he swept it across my clit. My hips slowly thrusted in response to his rubbing. *This is way better,* I thought, *than my fantasy in the office restroom.*

"What you're doing feels so good," I purred.

"Guess I should have been bolder before," he said, as his thumb's circling rose in speed. "I'm sorry."

"I should have been bolder too," I said between whimpers. "Let's both of us be bolder."

"Very well then. If I may confide in you now – though not about a personal fear but about something very naughty. This is my secret...it's my favorite way to make a woman cum."

As his thumb circled my clit, the palm shifted to one ass cheek – his hands were large enough that he could do that – and then his free palm cupped the other cheek. Gripping, he separated them, my nether hole on full display for him to see. The slight breeze tickled it.

Then a hot gob of his spit hit it, instantly warming the hole. The tip of a finger circled its rim then slipped in. I gasped.

He withdrew his finger then spit again and once again rubbed it around the rim and slowly pressed in until getting knuckle deep. My mouth opened wide to catch my breath, and he let his finger sit there for a long time, as his thumb teased my clit, gradually speeding up so I was close to climax then slowing down and pulling me from the brink, only to start his sweet torture again.

My juices dripped onto his thumb, and he wiped it onto his inserted finger, leaving me momentarily longing for him inside my pussy. His thumb returned to my clit, as he pumped his finger in and out of my ass, gradually increasing his pace as going deeper until it was all the way in.

Then, somehow he managed to move his finger and thumb in rhythm with one another, leaving me not knowing from where the next rising wave of pleasure was coming. One instant it was my clit, exposed thanks to his thumb's motions to the open air, the next instant it was from deep inside my vagina, a good five or six inches, some zone that past cocks rarely touched. I grew wetter and wetter so that I could feel my juices dripping along my thigh and the blanket below me, as he circled both my clit and some wall deep in my ass.

"Yes, yes, right...there," I gasped. "Don't...stop."

Every muscle in my body tensed, and then my body shook uncontrollably, as I screamed in ecstasy. Waves of pleasure rippled through me.

Thank you, Superman.

***

Matthew left his fingers frozen in place until my panting slowed and I'd fully caught my breath. Then he removed them and used the blanket's edge as a towel.

105

Finally I sat up. "I think I like when you're bold."

I locked my hands behind his head, and he released a pleasured moan, as I kissed his neck, his shoulders, his abs. My fingers trailed over the peaks and valleys of his muscles, and let my long hair tickle his chest and stomach, as I went licking and nipping at his physique until, growing impatient, I reached for his shorts' button and released his engorged cock straining against the fabric. I gently slid the zipper down then pulled them off him. He didn't wait and quickly wriggled his boxers down.

He was a giant of a man. There was no way he could be on top without crushing me.

"Lay back," I said.

He rested his body on the blanket and head on the pillow. I slithered and kissed my way up his leg then his abs and chest, until my pussy reached his thick cock. Planting my knees on both sides of his legs, I tucked my calves under my thighs and my toes under his legs then leaned down for a long kiss and sucked on his tongue while his hands kneaded my small breasts.

I slid up and down against his cock, letting it rub against my ass and between my pussy lips.

"I've never had sex on this boat," he said between kisses.

"It's time we christen it then."

He placed a hand on each of my ass cheeks, held me in place, and guided my pussy lips to the tip of his cock. Then my puckered pussy ground down on him. He let out a small grunt, as I fully engulfed it.

His cock throbbed inside me, as my hips gyrated on it. That wondrous sensation of being full overtook me. My heart quickened, and I slowly rode him cowgirl style, allowing myself to get used to his girth and length, relishing every pleasurable moment.

Then his hands on my ass held me still again, as he took charge and hammered in and out, filling me one instant, leaving me empty and longing for him the next. I gasped with each thrust, as he bucked like a bronco with me atop him, fucking me quick and fast. My mouth fell open trying to take in air, gasps and moans escaping from it, and I gripped his wrists to hold on to this bull of a man.

Our bodies glistened with sweat from the sun and our exertion, and I watched every muscle in his body grow increasingly tense. My breaths quickened. And then with one mighty thrust that went deeper than before, he froze and let out what sounded like a roar, as his hot cum shot into me.

An instant later, my neck arched, throwing my head back, and every particle in my body went rigid then disintegrated into a long, long moment of peace, as I came once more.

My hands loosened their grip on his wrists as my torso fell forward, my hair matted with sweat hanging from my face, and I tried to catch my breath. His cock slowly slid back and forth inside me, releasing whatever seed he had left, unable to relinquish the warmth and pleasure my pussy provided.

At last, his cock softened and slipped out, and I collapsed onto him. His arms wrapped around me, a hand caressing my lower back, as I molded my body into his. In moments, we were both asleep.

***

A burst of fireworks awoke us. With my eyes closed, I curled tighter against his warmth.

The sky boomed and rattled again, and with that we both were fully awake.

"The promised fireworks," Matthew said.

A spray of yellow, blue and red lit up the night sky.

"I preferred the earlier show," I said.

He chuckled, and I rolled away, looking for my clothes as stealing glances at his perfect arms, six-pack abs, and half-soft cock.

"What're you doing?" he said as staring me.

"Getting dressed – what if somebody sees me?"

He shrugged. "No one comes out here. And what if they did see you naked? You look super just as you are."

Matthew held out his arms, and I fell back into them. Watching the fireworks, we lay there on the blanket, exposed to one another and the world like Adonis and Aphrodite.

Opportunity

We took in Ryan at the last minute because Hannah flaked out on us a week before we got the keys. I wasn't angry about having a male roommate – though this was supposed to be an apartment just for us girls in our last year of college – but then Madison got her dream internship in another city and also flaked out, and there we were, just Ryan and me. We had no luck finding someone to replace Madison, so each of us had to work an extra part-time job to afford the place, and with classes on top of that, we were exhausted.

Because of our schedules, about the only time we ever saw one another was while watching football on Sunday afternoons. It turned out that we both liked the Falcons, and so there we sat, on opposite ends of the couch, cheering every touchdown and groaning over as many fumbles.

By the last Sunday of October, a while had passed since I'd gone out, and I found myself glancing over at Ryan like he were some handsome devil across the nightclub. And I have to admit, Ryan was damn good looking. Sporting broad shoulders and a toned body, a perpetual stubble lined his strong jawline. His light blue eyes were killer. And that cute butt of his, so round and firm, perfectly filled out his jeans.

But each time I peeked his way, I just as quickly turned back, telling myself that getting involved with my roommate – who I barely knew – would just complicate matters. I mean, how could we be boyfriend-girlfriend when we could get together only one afternoon a week? A relationship like that couldn't work. And if we did anything but weren't dating, what would happen if I brought a guy back home some night? Would Ryan get mad, move out? Then I'd lose the place.

Oh, who was I kidding, I finally thought, when was I ever going to bring a guy home? I'd been too tired to party since moving into that apartment.

I refocused on the game. The Falcons had fallen behind early but kept it close, always a big play away from taking the lead. Jack Blazer, our quarterback, was off target just when the team would get going. He was known as a gunslinger, but the new coach forced him to play within a system where he checked receivers in sequence, and if none were open, he was to throw it away. Admittedly, it had cut down on his interceptions from last year, but they weren't winning by broad margins either.

"Blazer's so much better when they let him improvise," I said.

"Maybe," Ryan responded, his hair dark and wavy, black T-shirt hugging his well-muscled arms. "But he's got to play within the system, Jennifer, or his teammates won't trust him. They'll never know what he's going to do next."

Just then Blazer threw a long pass to his guy, who caught it right on the sideline. We screamed "Yeahs!" and high-fived only for the referee to rule it incomplete because the receiver didn't get both feet down before going out of bounds.

"Oh no way!" I shouted at the same time Ryan hollered, "Are you blind, ref?" We looked at one another and shook our heads in disbelief.

Fortunately, the Falcons were able to snare a couple of hard-fought first downs and after a field goal got within a point. The momentum was swinging our way, and the players could feel it, too, as they'd slap the butt of the guy making a big play as running by him between downs. I have to admit, it was kind of a turn-on.

***

Despite being mad at Hannah and Madison, I missed them. I knew it didn't make sense, and so I did nothing about it. It's not like I had time to reach out anyway.

Then out of the blue one night, as I was falling asleep, Madison texted me.

How're you doing?

Alone and miserable and exhausted, I thought. At least Madison had a good reason to not take the apartment with me, so I responded, *Working a lot.*

Sorry. Madison knew she'd cast me aside. Then...*How is Ryan?*

Busy too. I yawned.

I met a guy. His name is Kaine. Super cute. Took me to the Bonavista, the restaurant that revolves.

Lucky you. Great.

A few moments passed before she replied. *We should get together when I'm back in town.*

I pondered whether or not I wanted to. Then, before I could decide, I fell asleep, phone still in hand.

***

The Falcons got the ball back with less than two minutes to go in the game. Blazer drove them down ably, connecting with his receivers like the plays called for, but he also overthrew them a couple of times. With time running out, enough for

111

maybe two plays, we still were not in field goal range. Blazer took the snap then suddenly protection broke down, and he scrambled. Locking eyes with a running back just a few yards away, Blazer pointed to a spot downfield then with a pass to that point hit him in stride. The back rushed down the field, weaving around defensive players for 10 yards then for 20, as we shouted him on. When he finally was taken down, close enough to try a long field goal, the Falcons called a time out with three seconds left on the clock.

The field goal team lined up. Ryan and I sat side by side, leaning forward together on the edge of the sofa, our hands clenched together in solidarity. The sandalwood scent of his aftershave filled my nostrils.

***

Madison never did text me back. I figured that was the end of it.

Then one morning I woke up to an email from Hannah. *Madison said you two weren't talking. I'm sorry about what happened. I feel that I'm the cause of it.*

Yeah, you sort of are, I thought.

When Austin asked me to move in with him, I didn't know what to do. But I love him and didn't want to cast any doubt in his mind about that.

So you abandoned us instead. Christ, Hannah, he was your boss.

We're engaged.

I didn't want to write something that sounded bitter. Yet if I was forgiving and we got together, I knew I'd only blow up at her.

So I went off to the shower to think about it. Then I went to class. By the end of the day, once home from work, I still hadn't responded.

The next morning, waking up tired from yet another night of not enough sleep, it slipped from my mind. With each passing day, not responding got easier.

***

For a few seconds, the kicker walked through his motions while a defensive player or two jumped up and down, warming up for a block. Then the two teams set, and the holder called for the ball. The center shot it back to him, and he placed it, as the kicker swung his leg forward. The ball sailed up over the defensive players' extended hands, and for what seemed like forever arced toward the posts until falling straight down the middle between the goal posts for the score.

We leaped up together, whooping and hollering – my body pulsed with joy, as it finally let loose – and we grabbed one another in a celebratory hug.

But when the moment came to pull away, we just stared for a long second into one another's eyes.

Our faces slowly moved closer to one another's, as if two merging clouds. He tilted his head slightly then stopped just before reaching my face and lightly grazed his lips over mine. The very tip of his tongue ran gently over my lower lip, and I opened my mouth a bit more. Suddenly his sweet tongue swirled in my mouth, as we pressed tighter against one another. The whole room spun. My arms slid around his neck to keep from falling over. I felt his growing erection, as our mouths pulled away for air. Something primal stirred deep within me.

My hands went to his shoulders, as I leaned in for another

113

kiss. Through our jeans I ground my pussy against his hard cock. His woodsy scent wound around me, and I luxuriated in the warmth of crushing my breasts against a man's hard chest.

But then I pulled away, had to clear my head. What the hell was I thinking? "I'm sorry – I can't – we shouldn't do this."

He looked away then nodded quickly. "No, you're right. It would be...well..."

"Yeah, it would be."

He sighed deep. "I think I need a cold shower."

I grinned then looked away.

He traipsed off to his room and then the bathroom. A loneliness filled me, as I ached for human touch, for the warmth that says *you are important, you are worthy of love.* You don't get that serving tables or studying ancient history. God damn you, Hannah and Madison, for leaving me.

I glanced up at the wall clock to see what time it was, and my eyes went big – not at how late it was but at the bathroom. Ryan had left the door open and had undressed. When he stepped into the shower, his round and perky butt flashed.

At the sound of the shower water, I stared at his silhouetted figure cleaning itself on the other side of the curtain. The mist of the hot water and the drops sliding down his arms softened his hard body. He brought both hands to his hair and rubbed in the shampoo. Even when not erect, he was well-endowed. I caressed my breasts.

The instant the shower water went off, my eyes shot back to the television screen, and my hands went under my butt. A moment or two passed, and he stepped out of the bathroom then stopped. I looked up at him.

His face shined red, as he held a white towel around his

waist. "Oh damn – I always shower after you've left, and I didn't think about closing the–"

"It's okay," I cut him off, the heat of embarrassment covering my face as well. "I...uh...didn't see anything."

He suppressed a frown. "Oh. I'm going to change. Wanna watch the Lions game?"

I hated the Lions, the most inept team out there. "Um...sure."

He headed to his room, and I watched his cute butt, only partially covered by his towel, sway toward his room. My heart hammered faster, as a pressure built within my core.

I pointed the remote at the TV but paused. The on field reporter was interviewing Jack Blazer.

"I've got to give it to our guys," he said, his hair matted with sweat, "they really hung in there. When the opportunity presented itself, they came through. That's what this game is all about, taking hold of your opportunities."

He gave the sign of the cross, pointed to the sky, then trotted off.

I clicked the remote to the channel carrying the Lions game.

Oh fuck the Lions, I told myself; the only roar I want to hear was from a man cumming inside me after I'd fucked his dick long and hard. Time to pull a Jack Blazer.

I went down the hall and stood in his doorway, admiring the taut muscles of his backside, as he reached down to his bed for his T-shirt.

He turned around and, entirely naked, stumbled back. "Jennifer?"

With that, I walked straight up to him, dropped to my knees, and took his cock in my hand. Slowly my lips made their way over his cockhead, first up one side then the other, letting my hot breath and moist lips engulf part of him while the other was left in the dry cold anxiously waiting for my attention. He hardened instantly.

"Jennifer, we shouldn–"

Ignoring him, I grasped the base of his cock, slowly wrapped my lips around its head, then swirled the tip of my tongue just under his cockhead. Looking up at him with a mischievous glint in my eye, I licked the crown of his cock then kissed it. My free hand glided up his thigh and gripped it, the nails digging into the skin, as my lips wrapped about the cock. I tightened my grip on his shaft and then swallowed half of it. Slowly pulling away, I glanced up; his eyes were half shut and lips slightly parted, as if he were dizzy.

I'd won. Or rather something *inside me* had won.

As I took him in and out of my mouth, his large hand caressed the back of my head.

I kept the head of his cock in my mouth as my thumb and forefinger stroked down his shaft with little pressure and then back up, squeezing as I went. His breathing grew heavier, and his earthy scent rose as sweat beaded on him. I softly caressed his balls while my mouth bobbed up and down on his cock. The saltiness of his precum covered my tongue.

I pulled my head away from his cock, and he placed his hands beneath my underarms and lifted me to my feet. As his hard cock grazed my jeans, he slowly rolled my shirt up, exposing the waist, then over my head and somewhere into the corner of his room it went.

When both hands found and caressed my breasts, his fingers pinched my right nipple. I let out a soft moan.

I reached behind my back, unlatched the bra, and shrugged

the straps off my shoulders. As my breasts fell free, he circled his tongue about them until reaching and flicking, several times, each nipple. My knees weakened and eyes closed.

As he worked on each nipple, his hands unsnapped my jeans and tugged them down past my ankles. I stepped out of them.

Then, holding the small of my back with his large hand, Ryan kissed up the side of my neck until reaching my ear. He whispered, "I've wanted you since we first met two months ago."

I pulled away, and as turning around, latched my thumbs inside the top band of my panties, pushing down first one side, revealing my crack and a butt cheek, then the other side so my ass was fully exposed. I left the panties at my thighs, bunched into a thin, vulnerable line. I've wanted him that long too.

Ryan placed an arm around me and with one hand kneaded my breast. As he gently pinched the nipple, his other hand palmed a butt cheek. My eyes closed, my breathing deepened, my knees barely held me up, as he glided me around, almost as if in a dance, so I faced the bed.

He stood behind me, his hard cock pressed against the crack of my ass, one hand squeezing a breast with a nipple between two fingers. "You are perfect," he whispered in my ear.

His hand gently pressed my back, pushing me downward so I stood bent over, tummy on the mattress. Then he dropped to his knees.

His thumbs pressed my ass cheeks just above my butthole, then the fingers reached to where my inner thighs met the bed, and he caressed upward, pinching my labia until the fingertips reached just below his thumbs. With each stroke, as his fingers reached my ass, my released labia unfurled farther until my moistness dripped upon his hand and my swollen clit protruded from its opening. Breathing hard, I wiggled, trying to brush my clit against him.

Then he thrust two fingers into my pussy while a finger of his other hand rested on my butthole; I dared not move lest it slip inside. I gasped with each thrusts, which only encouraged him to quicken his pace. I sank into the pleasure, hips rocking with the motion. OK, I thought, I may need to write Hannah and Madison thank you cards.

My hands grasped the sheets while my pussy arched up to meet his fingers. The bottom half of my legs tensing with each thrust. Then my ass tightened as my whole lower body squirmed. I bit down hard on the sheet.

A ticklish, hot wave rose from the center of my pussy and rippled out toward my fingertips and toes.

Ryan stopped thrusting, let me enjoy the moment. Then he stood. His hands gripped my waist, as his cock sat at my pussy's entrance. In a sports announcer voice, Ryan said, "He steps up under center, ready to take the snatch."

I broke out laughing.

Then he eased into me, and I gasped in pleasure. My hips rose to greet him. Pushing a little more, he slowly slid further inside me, inch by inch.

He paused as we relished the sensation of my body sheathing him.

I wondered why we hadn't done this a month ago when the Falcons won their first game.

A final thrust pushed him to the hilt.

With agonizing slowness, he drew his cock back then pressed in again, allowing his large member to stretch me with intense pleasure. My hips met his. Each time I tried to increase the pace, he backed off, leaving me almost empty.

After three failed attempts, I realized what he wanted.

Ryan swept his hand across his glorious cock, only its head in my entrance, then swiped my pussy juices down the crack of my ass. His wet finger rimmed my netherhole.

I moaned as my neck arched up.

Then his finger pressed into the hole. My ass tightened, and his free hand firmly pulled a butt cheek away from the other. His finger pushed until it was knuckle deep. My hips gyrated on his finger until it was all the way in, and then he thrust his cock fully inside me.

The walls of my pussy contracted around his cock, as some fantastical energy pent up inside rose in me like a wave, and then I let go, let that suddenly very real energy sweep over me.

He grunted loudly, as if in triumph, as I felt his warm seed fill me.

In the same instant, a second wave swept through me, and my body collapsed against the bed and trembled.

Ryan withdrew and climbed onto the mattress, his muscled body clad only in sweat, then offered his hands to help me climb up. I took them and rested my head on his chest, the curves of my body hugging his. My heart slowed and muscles relaxed, as placing a hand on his broad chest. He lay stretched out, his broad shoulders and chest angling to a narrow waist then widening to well-hewn legs, his spent cock only half-erect but still beautiful.

My head tilted back. His light blue eyes peacefully stared at the ceiling.

As his fingers gently stroked my hair, I looked him in the

eyes. "I didn't know you felt this way about me."

"Haven't you seen the way I've been looking at you these past nine weeks?" he said.

"I guess I've been too tired to notice."

He nodded. "Maybe I've been too tired to do more than look."

"Are you tired now?"

He shook his head.

I grinned then crawled on top of him, rubbing my wet slit against his cock, hardening it. "Good. Because the second quarter is about to begin."

If you got a little excited from reading this book, please take a few moments to write a review of it:

amazon.com/dp/1948872439

XOXOXO – Emily

Interview with Emily

Q: How did you come to write this collection?
A: They're an outgrowth of my spanking stories. When researching the spanking fetish, some of the writings and discussions would naturally turn to anal play in general – rimming, fingering, anal sex, anal orgasms. I gathered a lot of material for stories in this collection. Spanking and anal play are very different fetishes, but I found a lot of the psychology is the same.

Q: Did you write the stories in the order they appear?
A: No, I started with the "more acceptable" forms of the fetish. "Opportunity" was the first story written, and it's really not about the fetish as other something else, but it has anal fingering in it. "Red is the Rose" was the last piece I wrote, and that's about someone who already is heavily into anal sex.

Q: Which story was the most difficult to write?
A: Good question! I think they were all equally challenging. Actually, "Partners" probably was the *least* difficult to write. It just came to me over a couple of days. In fact, I was so in the zone that as soon as I finished it, I immediately wrote a prequel to it, even though I was supposed to be working on stories for this anthology.

Q: Do you have a favorite from the collection?
A: That's like asking a parent who their favorite child is, lol. I like each one for different reasons. I hope that "All the Way" is

liked the most by readers, as it explores how our society's negative attitudes toward anal play affect the emotional state of the main character, who's a typical, everyday person. This fetish isn't something that makes you an "abnormal" person; many so called "normal" people have fetishes. I also hope people like "Partners" and "Atonement" because those two pieces have some neat twists in them.

Q: For you, what makes a great story?
A: For me, I have to want to know what is going to happen next; I want the author's storytelling talents to force me to read the next paragraph and to turn the page. There are at least trillions of ways to achieve that, but it comes down to creating interesting characters engaged in an intriguing conflict (plot) and being tightly written. Getting the right POV that best serves the story also is vital. I'd add that for me, I want the author to make me think about stuff like ethics or the nature of human existence, so I'm looking for a theme as well. And yes, you can do all of that in erotica just as much as you can do it in literary fiction or fantasy or sci-fi or any other genre.

Q: This is your fourth anthology. How do you feel that you've grown as a writer?
A: When I started out long before I was published, I didn't really understand the craft of writing. I had a good grasp of spelling, punctuation and grammar as well as a little imagination – which probably is why my high school English teachers told me I should be a writer – but I didn't exactly understand how to write tightly, how to pen engaging dialogue, how to show rather than tell, how to weave the intricacies of

character development into a good plot, how to choose the best point of view for my story, and a thousand other things. A really good editor mentored me in all of this, and now I feel like I can write a halfway decent story.

Q: Would you say your stories fit firmly into the "real world" or are they escapism?
A: Both but leaning heavily toward "real world." More of the stories explore sexual issues that real people face. At the same time, some of the sex is probably a little too fantastic to be true, but then again…

Q: What do you enjoy most about writing your stories?
A: Being creative delivers a lot of personal fulfillment. Imagine being a kid with a coloring book – except you also get to draw the black lines that you have to color within. That's what being a writer is like. You're using your imagination, you're overcoming multiple challenges, and you're wielding power. I love all of that.

Q: Will you write more anal stories?
A: Most definitely. I have enough story ideas for about three more anthologies. All of them are started and in various stages of completion.

Bonus Excerpt
from "Spanking Tales"

He sat on the edge of his bed. "Come here."

I rose, and when I got to Clayton, his hand grabbed my wrist and the other my shoulder, then he pulled me down so my tummy was across his lap. I let out a yelp.

"Separate your legs," he said.

As I did so, my wet pussy gaped, fully exposed before him.

He pressed his palm into my shoulder blades, holding me in place as his other hand reached for something. I was able to turn my head just enough to see he'd grabbed a wooden spoon from beneath a pillow.

Hmmm, this should be interesting. No one has ever diddled my clit with a wooden spoon before.

Then *snap!* as the wooden spoon slapped against my ass, and I jerked upward on his lap. His hand was strong, though, and held me in place.

"This is for not being honest," he said.

Snap!

"Uh!" I winced then grit my teeth, as he struck my ass again.

My ass burned with pain, and the heat only rose, as he kept slapping it with the spoon. With each strike, I rose a little higher off his lap until his forearm pressed into my upper back, so that his weight held me down. My heart pounded, and a month went by in an instant.

Snap!

"This is for betraying your best friend," he said.

Snap!

My hand grabbed his legs, dug in.

"Why would you betray your best friend?" he asks.

Because I wanted to see if you were really like what she said, I wanted to say. But that would have been a lie, probably earning me a few more whacks.

So I lied.

"That's not the reason why," he said.

Snap!

"Is it?"

Snap!

My nipples hardened. "No," I whimpered.

Snap!

"Then what was it?"

"Because I wanted to know what it was like to be...spanked."

Snap!

"And what's it like?"

Snap!

His voice rose. "And what's it like?"

My ass sizzled from the hard smacks I'd so craved. "I'm excited...like I've never been before...like I've always *wanted* to be."

"Finally, you're telling the truth. Your juices are dripping down my thigh, you're so turned on. Have you had enough?"

Despite that my ass burned with pain, I suddenly felt...*comfortable*. Yes, that was the word for it. *Comfortable*. "I deserve...more."

Snap!

I breathed in through my clenched teeth as my haunches shook frantically.

He gave me four more whacks then lifted his forearm from

my back. "Get on the bed, tummy down."

I wobbled onto the bed, holding my hand to my butt, feeling the heat rising from it. I laid down.

"Put your ass up in the air."

I shifted my knees closer to my waist, lifting my red butt. I heard his zipper being undone then his pants and belt buckle hitting the floor. He stepped out of his boxers and got on his knees behind me, ran the head of his cock against my slit.

"Your ass looks so damn hot all red like that." Clayton slowly slid in then almost all the way out. I moaned, bit my lower lip.

His cock pressed back in, and soon his thrusts fell into an urgent rhythm.

"Look back at me," he commanded. "Look back at me while I fuck you."

I looked over my shoulder at him, locking onto his gray eyes, groaning with each thrust. My eyes closed in pleasure.

"Keep them open," he said. "Keep looking at me."

I did, though with great difficulty.

"Ride my cock," he said and stopped thrusting.

My thighs and hips pushed me back on his cock then pistoned on it. His cock felt better than any fingers ever could. I picked up speed as he stood there, his head arched back, moaning.

An instant later, he pulled out and shot his hot load across my still burning ass cheeks.

Every one of my muscles tensed, as I shouted "Holy fucking God" and spasmed. For several seconds, my body floated in a pool of warmth, then I collapsed to the mattress.

Catching his breath, Clayton stumbled over to his dresser and grabbed something. A moment later, he squirted lotion onto my ass cheeks, cooling the burn. His large hand stirred the lotion with his cum, mixing it, then rubbed the concoction into my skin.

– from "Curiouser and Curiouser"
anthologized in "Spanking Tales"

"Spanking Tales" is available in paperback, Kindle ebook, and audiobook at Amazon.com.

About Emily Rooks

Emily Rooks is the author of erotic romance that sizzles with passion and tension. Her stories explore sexuality from a woman's perspective and feature strong female protagonists. She holds a bachelor's degree in literature and creative writing and resides in Los Angeles.

True Lust Titles

Anthologies
- Backdoor Tales
- Spanking Tales
- Spanking Tales, Volume II
- Young Studs

Short Stort Standalones
- Atonement
- Chalk
- Opportunity
- Star Pupil
- Supergirl
- Venus Fly Trap

Better Sex Guidebooks
- Essential Foreplay Tips

Connect with Emily

BlueSky
emilyrookstruelust.bsky.social

Facebook
(limited posts)
facebook.com/EmilyRooksTrueLust

Goodreads
goodreads.com/user/show/146421357-emily-rooks

Literotica
literotica.com/authors/EmilyRooks/works/stories

Pinterest
pinterest.com/emilyrookstruelust

Website
emilyrookstruelust.com

X/Twitter
x.com/EmilyRooksTrueL